FACE

Books by Jaspreet Singh

NOVELS
Face (2022)
Helium (2013)
Chef (2008)

MEMOIR
My Mother, My Translator (2021)

POETRY
How to Hold a Pebble (2022)
November (2017)

SHORT STORIES
Seventeen Tomatoes: Tales from Kashmir (2004)

FACE

A Novel of the Anthropocene

Jaspreet Singh

BRINDLE
AND GLASS

Brindle & Glass
An imprint of TouchWood Editions
touchwoodeditions.com

Edited by Claire Philipson
Copy edited by Meg Yamamoto
Proofread by Senica Maltese
Cover design by Tree Abraham
Cover illustration: With permission of the Royal Ontario Museum and
Parks Canada © ROM. Illustration credit: Marianne Collins
Interior design by Sydney Barnes

CATALOGUING DATA AVAILABLE FROM LIBRARY AND ARCHIVES CANADA
ISBN 9781927366974 (softcover)
ISBN 9781927366981 (electronic)

TouchWood Editions acknowledges that the land on which we live and work is within the traditional territories of the Lkwungen (Esquimalt and Songhees), Malahat, Pacheedaht, Scia'new, T'Sou-ke and W̱SÁNEĆ (Pauquachin, Tsartlip, Tsawout, Tseycum) peoples.

We acknowledge the financial support of the Government of Canada through the Canada Book Fund and the Canada Council for the Arts, and of the Province of British Columbia through the British Columbia Arts Council and the Book Publishing Tax Credit.

This book was produced using FSC®-certified, acid-free papers, processed chlorine free, and printed with soya-based inks.

Printed in Canada at Friesens

26 25 24 23 22   1 2 3 4 5

It is harder to rid oneself of ghosts that have been in
your own rooms.
—*Javier Marías*

The Anthropocene will not go away when we go away.
—*Jan Zalasiewicz*

Aunt Lina said that spirits existed . . . in people's ears,
in the eyes when eyes looked inside and not out, in the
voice as soon as it begins to speak, in the head when it
thinks . . .
—*Elena Ferrante*

If we burn all the fossil fuels, the ice sheets almost surely
will melt entirely, with the final sea level rise about
75 meters (250 feet), with most of that possibly occur-
ring within a time scale of centuries. . . . After the ice
is gone, would Earth proceed to the Venus syndrome, a
runaway greenhouse effect that would destroy all life on
the planet, perhaps permanently?
—*James Hansen*

There is no end
To what a living world
Will demand of you.
—*Octavia E. Butler*

O

"Story is our only boat for sailing on the river of time," says Ursula Le Guin. "No boat is safe."

Story is our only boat for sailing on the river of time. No boat is safe, but our boats change the river.

Our boats have been changing the river for a while now. The scientists just conveyed to us. Story is a geological agent.

Imagining

I

In this new epoch most stories rhyme with crime. Or with witnesses (i.e., ghosts or ghosts-to-be in layers of rocks). Because I am doing the telling, this story will involve both at once. Sadly, this puts limits on my freedom. For (after making the narrative choice) I, too, must follow standard rules and conventions, and solve the problem of beginning. One can either begin with a character imagining their own demise and the aftermath in the biosphere, or begin with someone already gone but unable to stop intervening in planetary affairs. One can begin with a compelling, beckoning voice that tries to make contact with the reader right from the first page. Something like this—

2

When I see a child playing with plastic dinosaurs these days the tape of memory starts rolling. Our kitchen window had a little hole slightly bigger than three swollen fingers, and through that hole a squirrel would make its way in. My parents asked a carpenter to block the hole with a piece of plastic, and from that day on the one-eyed squirrel and I would look at each other's faces for long periods of time through plastic.

The squirrel was trying to say something to me. I understood completely. It needed my help. But I could not help, not even in a small way.

I have never looked at a human face from so close and for so long. Perhaps it is more accurate to say that it only happened once. Only once did I look at a human face the way I had looked at the squirrel and there was no glass partition or plastic between us. I don't know about you, but for me things that only happen once feel as if they simply did not happen.

■ ■ ■

The lights turned red again and a few random people in a downtown street—the ones who got clogged on one side, the ones who made a slight effort—might have witnessed something strange going on inside the second floor of a building. Their eyes might have rested on two women inside. Perhaps for a brief unhurried second.

The women were sitting anomalously close to each other, not saying a word, not gesturing, simply staring at each other's faces. Both were at once the observer and the observed. Two strangers who had just met.

They did not even know each other's names; so far neither one of them was aware that within the next fifty-one days one of them was going to die.

■ ■ ■

The women continued face to face for seven or eight more minutes. This means some four or five batches of randomly accumulated people at the intersection might have witnessed the event, especially the ones who made an effort.

One of the women was called Lucia. The other one was me, Lila. Even when I was back in India my parents had reduced my name, Lilawati, to Lila; correct pronunciation: Leela.

At that point in time Lucia and I were sitting in black folding chairs, somewhat precarious, in a bright room on the second floor of an old sandstone building in Western Canada. Calgary, to be specific, a prairie city six hours south of oil sand deposits, a city that can no longer be called small.

It was the last exercise the workshop instructor had given us, a surprise. He called them *games*. A middle-aged white man with fitful hair and a conspicuously mediocre dress sense; cold blue eyes; someone known in his profession, but not well known. He had divided the group of sixteen into almost random pairs and asked us to sit very close to each other (half a metre apart) and pay attention to the other's face.

The pairs had formed as man-man or man-woman or woman-woman. But at that point in time none of this difference mattered. Because we were all there with a well-defined purpose: to learn to write creatively. Our age variation was anywhere from twenty to fifty. The instructor made us do two-page writing exercises after little activities, some in small groups and some in pairs. Some activities, like face watching, had the power to make us uncomfortable.

He had warned us beforehand. If it really makes you uncomfortable, feel free to stop the exercise at that very moment and step out of the room for a while. Now that I think about it, I did feel uncomfortable watching Lucia's face for what seemed like an interminable amount of time, but not uncomfortable enough to walk out of the room. I remained seated, our knees only a few millimetres apart.

We had complete freedom in face watching. A writing exercise was going to follow. We were not supposed to share the stuff, raw or polished, not with our pair and not even with the instructor. This way no one would be able to influence what we wrote.

How to watch? someone in the group demanded before the exercise began. No words, no laughter while observing, the instructor explained. Other than that there were no rules. If you just end up writing two or three pages about the corner of an eye or the curl of a lip, that is perfectly fine with me, he said. Or how you felt or how you made the other feel. Anything goes.

As the exercise began, I thought that I had never done this kind of observing—not even with the people I was involved with intimately, not even with family members. There was a phase in my life when I would look at the face of my then boyfriend from very close and for a long time while he lay on the bed. But that was a different situation and I would abruptly stop when he woke up.

Lucia's face—even as I stared—would be difficult to fix permanently in my mind. I paid close attention to her eyes and lips, the mole on her left cheek, the moderately defiant shape of her brow and nose; I found myself giving silent words to the colour of her skin, its texture. She had short but voluminous hair, like a younger Hannah Arendt, but the face was its own unique thing. Eyebrows radically different from each other, one arched and the other straight, and yet this did not take away any symmetry.

In my mind a vague shape called "my partner's face" planted itself, but the details changed constantly as if there was not a single solution to some grand puzzle.

If anything I felt the face had a persistent voice and was trying to say something.

"Don't betray me," it was saying. "Now that you have looked at me for so long and from so close, do not betray me." The more I looked, the more I felt responsible for the person whose face I was looking at.

I don't know how Lucia saw my face . . . I had to wait for fifty-one days to begin answering that simple question.

The only thing that is clear to me now and that was clear then was that neither the instructor nor Lucia nor I knew that soon in a matter of a few months one of us would not make it. I don't want to give the impression that the phrase "not make it" is any different from "die." I say it because at that point in time when we were sitting extremely close to each other, death was the farthest thing from our minds, for we were filled with life (as they say).

I was cheerful because of good news at work. And Lucia was more or less in a similar state of contentedness. I felt she was repressing a big smile; if the instructor had not imposed strict rules she might have even burst into laughter.

Confidently, he kept wandering from pair to pair throughout the exercise and finally announced in a loud voice from a faraway corner that our time was up. "Feel free to stop slowly; some of you might not be able to stop quickly," he said. "Stop as you wish." Someone let out a sigh. The chairs moved a bit and most of us began the writing assignment. Only eight or nine minutes had passed during the exercise, but it seemed like an eternity.

■ ■ ■

Some half an hour later the workshop ended officially and the group started breaking. An email list passed around the room, but neither Lucia nor I put our names on it. We had just started a little conversation—perhaps she wanted to invite me to coffee (I would have liked it)—when Lucia noticed a man waiting for her at the doorway.

The same man had dropped her off earlier during the day. I had arrived ten minutes late, and she had arrived a few minutes later. Now he was back. Without saying goodbye, she rushed in his direction. It was clear she was happy to see him. So was he. Both conveyed this info openly to all those who made an effort in the room. Silently, I observed their healthy or seemingly healthy relationship from a distance. Only silence can observe such things.

The man was wearing a long navy blue overcoat with buttons open. Curly salt and pepper hair. His glasses could have been Ray-Ban. By the time Lucia made it to him he had already isolated her sports-style jacket from the heap. He gently helped her get into it, arranged her scarf, and, as a final reward, planted an intimate peck somewhere on her face.

He was almost the same height as Lucia and Lucia was not wearing heels that day. She waved at me with both hands and then they left. From the doorway the man most likely did not make out who his partner was waving at.

I had a feeling that I knew that face.

But I could not place him. I could not tell if I had met him in a professional or a personal capacity. Perhaps I knew him when he was a lot younger. Perhaps I had imagined that the young man would acquire such a face in middle age.

But I was not sure. Perhaps I was already inventing reasons to see her again. Some other participants came to me to say goodbye. One hugged me for no reason. From the window I looked at the street, the intersection where random strangers would come together waiting for the light to turn. And not far from the intersection there was a train station. LRT. Lucia was on the platform now holding unmittened hands with the man; they were waiting for a local train. Something about them made it clear that they were taking the train not because they had stopped using the car, but because their car was parked just outside downtown. Something about them suggested that they lived in the suburbs in one of those desired houses with a two-car garage and three co-lour-coded garbage bins and little aspen and ash trees in the garden. The moment I saw them from this vantage point, I made a split-second decision, exited the building, and ran toward the approaching train. They didn't notice me. They were still far away and the place was reason-ably crowded by Calgary standards. By the time I made it on the platform, their train had already left, heading southwest.

Slowly I retraced my path through the street and returned back to the workshop room, my jacket still in there. Almost everyone had left. Only the instructor and two keen students, noisier than the entire city and much younger than me, remained. I observed advanced stages of flirtation. They were headed for a drink.

"I forgot something," my voice said more to myself than to them, and I made it to the chairs where Lucia and I had been sitting. The chairs were still facing each other. Right beneath her chair there was a little object, not mine. I picked it up.

When Lucia was observing my face, perhaps after the second or the third minute, she had crossed her legs the other way. Obviously she felt a bit uncomfortable then. Without stopping the activity she had picked up her handbag from the carpet and put it on her knees. She dug around in it with one hand, searching for something specific. I don't know if she found the exact thing, but she moved the handbag back to the carpet. From that moment on, she kept the small stone in her hand to calm herself, or so I thought.

"Did you find what you lost?" asked the instructor.

"Yes," I said, putting the stone in my pocket.

3

I returned to my lugubrious two-bedroom apartment and without tidying up any disorder began expanding the hurriedly written fragment—*Face of a Stranger*—I'd started during the workshop. The inner block was no longer there, and time passed by quickly. The long weekend, a religious holiday (celebrated in Canada by two large ethnic groups, English and French), had just started. Around midnight I felt extremely thirsty and warmed a cup of water in the microwave with mustard stains. Twenty minutes later came pangs of hunger. The pears and plums in the basket looked as if they had no intention to beckon me. So I fried a large brown egg.

I work as a journalist for a provincial magazine. A science journal, to be specific. Sixty-five thousand readers. Technically I am supposed to inhabit an open-concept space at the magazine office—the entire sixth floor of a nine-storey building. But there are days I simply work from home or go to a public library or a café with a laptop.

Because of my line of work I have many encounters

with scientists, above-average or brilliant men and women, mostly geologists and climate systems experts these days, and this has been wonderful (and at times not so wonderful, especially when I realize their limitations). It gladdens me that I do this job and do not focus on the doings of politicians.

The articles I write these days have moved beyond the so-called cool stuff, like "Is there life on Venus?" I no longer use catchy sound bites from celebrity scientists, phrases like "To make an apple pie from scratch, you must first invent the universe." These days I am more and more interested in shadowing individual researchers. This automatically leads me to minor epics in the labs. I do extended interviews. Each week I become a "specialist" (doesn't matter how transient) in a particular area and play the role of "interpreter" for the general public.

I am a better journalist than many others of my generation because I am not afraid of taking sides. When interacting with scientists, I side with the general public, and when interacting with the public, I privilege the voice of the scientists. The aspiration is to make sure both groups feel well represented, even when one or the other is proven wrong.

Mostly I skip going online (unless it involves essential research or emails). Colleagues young and old call me old-fashioned for "wilfully" keeping Twitter and Facebook at bay. In my mind there are two reasons I get to ignore atmospheric disturbances brought about by peer pressure. (1) The editor admires the reality-check quality of my work.

(2) My growing reputation: I have won eight National Magazine Awards and the Science Writing Award. The Science Writing Award is more prestigious; a distinguished jury handed it to me at a ceremony in Ottawa for a series of articles on ancient DNA studies and migrations.

The reason I participated (after months of planning) in the fiction workshop is straightforward: I would like to learn more about how to write about people. I would like to enter a character's consciousness, open the so-called black box. I know how to write about heat and thermodynamics, about Schrödinger's cat, phosphine, mitochondrial DNA, cyanobacteria, nanobots, symbiosis, and endangered rare earth elements used in mobile phones to display bright colours. Yttrium, terbium and dysprosium. I can detail juicy stories about *Tiktaalik*, and mangrove ecosystems, and the spread of mountain pine beetle that leaves millions of trees starved and dead. I can analyze laboratory slang and old-school geologist jokes. I can do flawless pieces on *sapiens* migrations that might have occurred some seventy thousand years ago right after the Toba supervolcanic eruption, or interpret sublime and beautiful archaic walking-whale fossils in the Himalayas. I can write glowing reports on Nora Noffke's extraordinary work (MISS), I know how to compose exploratory essays about 3-D scanning and printing, also the wilful racial and gender code bias in facial-recognition software and other artificial-intelligence algorithms sold by tech companies. But I need help, serious help, writing about real people, real human beings and their relationships.

I would like to learn how to make real living breathing people live and breathe on a page.

Of course, when I do journalism, I report the activities of people; scientists are also people, but I end up depicting them in a standard way and that standard way has severe limitations.

When the magazine was in the process of hiring me, the selection committee asked that dreaded what-colour-is-your-parachute question.

"What are your *weaknesses*?"

"I have got only one."

"What is it?"

"Not being able to work nine to five!"

"Meaning you are unreliable," the managing editor misinterpreted.

"You can rely on my reliability," I clarified. "I start long before 9:00 AM and stop long after 5:00 PM. I am ever ready to take on multiple projects on short notice and follow them through, and I rarely shy away from experts in the field. You will be hiring the ideal person for conducting interviews. Someone adept at fishing out information from deep waters."

The confession was true, more or less, yet the day they sent me the job offer I could not help but laugh at myself for having mastered finally the banality of North American lingo.

Often such insignificant memory traces come back to me for no particular reason. There are traces I call "signals" and traces I call random "noise." Less unhappy are people who can clearly distinguish between a signal and noise.

■ ■ ■

Lucia's stone was trying to say something. After a lot of close looking and tactile observations I placed it on my desk. Embedded in the stone: a fossil. Most likely a *Pikaia*. Nothing extraordinary. Such deep time exists in abundance in Yoho National Park in the Canadian Rockies. Lucia's stone could have come from the Burgess Shale quarry, the soft-bodied fossil site full of "two-inch worms" from the Cambrian age (~500 million years ago). Only a three-hour drive from Calgary.

■ ■ ■

Next morning the weather was a bit warped. Before making coffee (no cream, no sugar), I dispatched a short email to the writing instructor. I obviously didn't write, "One participant woke up fussing about beautiful Lucia," nor did I hint at my curiosity about the vague shape of a man who had come to collect her. I could not shake the feeling he was known to me from some other era. As if I had seen his face fifty or five thousand times and each time it made me uncomfortable.

I had never seen Lucia before. Perhaps once, actually. In a local magazine. When my father last visited Calgary, he encountered a diasporic magazine at a grocery store.

It was free; he brought it home. Such magazines are often filled with thousands of hurriedly made ads and low-res photographs. Flipping through I saw ads for cars, houses, furniture, lawyers, life workshops, cooking classes, dance and yoga lessons, fortune tellers, etc. A page was missing. Page 25 carried photos of a gala event held near Heritage Drive. The black-and-white gala photos had no captions; perhaps it was expected that the magazine readers already knew the names of the luminaries. Lucia was one of them. Posing as if she naturally belonged to the photo. But I am not sure. The same man was standing next to her in one of those photos, trying to blend in.

While drinking coffee I made three failed attempts to locate the diasporic magazine in my study. The piles of shiny mainstream city magazines I had gathered didn't seem to contain it. Most mainstream magazines were an excess of silly little vignettes that belonged to the bygone Holocene epoch. Shuffling through shallow drawers and storage boxes, strange thoughts flickered within me. A rush of inner chaos ended up creating more disorder in my apartment than my senses usually allow. *Not today. Not today.*

■ ■ ■

It was a four-day-long-bridge weekend. Ample time for the predator instructor to prey on the two younger students from the previous evening. I waited with dwindling patience for his response to my email. I later left a message on his office machine. "It is urgent."

He phoned back, bluntly saying that he could not give away a student's email, but it was possible to "facilitate an exchange of information."

"Of course."

"What did you find?"

"Best to disclose it directly to the owner."

"Your name? Your partner's name?"

He sounded a bit hungover. Mispronounced my name right after I provided it. I ignored the microaggression. Something more important was at stake. I described the place where we sat, the clothes she was wearing, a few features of her face, her handbag. Yellow Dolce & Gabbana.

"She doesn't know my name, and vice versa. We both arrived late and missed the participant introductions session," I told him.

"There were so many of you," he said. "Does she have an accent?"

"But everyone has an accent," I said.

"Something else? Something unusual? By any chance, does she exhibit problems with the future tense? Is she the one who skips 'will'? Does she use 'I call tomorrow,' instead of 'I will call tomorrow'?"

I paused. This insightful thought had not crossed my mind before.

"Perhaps. Perhaps."

"The name is Lucia."

■ ■ ■

The kitchen sink needed a thorough clean. Wearing rubber gloves I polished its surfaces, carefully removing the green layers of patina that had formed on the faucet. For a change I tried to do "fun" soul-relaxing stuff. I tried watching grainy old black-and-white films from Japan on my laptop.

But restored-and-digitized films from Japan only made me think obliquely and even more obsessively about Lucia. I thought about the black folding chairs, the room where we met; I thought about the old sandstone heritage building in which the room was. In the early 1900s city officials had used stone from the Paskapoo Formation to construct many fire-resistant structures downtown. My cellphone translated *Paskapoo* from Cree to English as *blind man*.

By late afternoon the skies cleared up and the city started drying itself with the usual speed. I took longish strolls through bare, unleafy streets. During one random outing I went into a used bookstore (the one that lacks the smell of old books and mould) to check if they had the English translation of author Liu Cixin's *The Three-Body Problem*.

A man in a graphic T-shirt accompanied me to the very back, muttering in a heavy British accent, "Don't forget this is Calgary."

"But this is one of the finest bookstores in the city."

"Even the finest relies on what the locals bring us."

I liked his sardonic face. Two contradictory things flashed within me: a long-forgotten word in Sanskrit that means "genuine lasting happiness independent of circumstances," and the feeling that this was the face of a man who (always) chooses his partners badly.

I began scanning translated books. My anxious hands were going through an earlier novel by Liu Cixin when the owner turned on a streaming device and clever fugue-like music filled the room with a serene energy.

Bach.

A lyrical voice announced "Classic FM," a radio station based in London.

"So what keeps *you* here in our wondrous city?" I asked at the cash register.

The store owner, my fellow migrant, looked right through my face before uttering the word *sanity* in a well-preserved British accent.

"Insanity," he corrected himself.

I let the pause grow.

"My seventeen-year-old doesn't talk to me. But to live in some other city far from my son is unimaginable."

I did not know what to say. His eyes blinked two or three times faster than normal. He had provided more information than I was after. Men rarely do such a thing.

Back in the apartment I played the tape of recent memory while doing my weekly laundry. I spread the clothes on two stands in the balcony and turned on Classic FM. The website demanded a British postal code. I knew one. I began flipping through the Liu Cixin book. Hard sci-fi. Rich imagination. Not as rich as the imagination of my all-time favourite author, Octavia E. Butler.

Cixin's aliens—I found—more convincing than his female characters. The first half of the paperback was marked generously with a faint orange highlighter. Every other page dog eared. Turned down with exactitude to give it the aura of a perfect ruin. The second half looked untouched. Smell of damaged fascination.

"Isn't the music blissful?" the serene and beautiful voice continued on Classic FM. "And this one is for Michael, who has been living as an expat in Calgary, Canada, for eighteen years. We will meet again. Soon he will return home."

■ ■ ■

Next morning the streets were as dry as a bone. I strolled back to the bookstore, filled with a natural curiosity about the owner's name. A curiosity propelled by mild attraction. Perhaps I was drawn more to the graphic T-shirt, Bach, and the radio coincidence in my apartment.

This time I bought three books. Cixin's *The Dark Forest*. Octavia E. Butler's *Parable of the Sower*. And Stephen Jay Gould's *Wonderful Life*. One of the pages in the book was in Hindi. Gould had reproduced the cover of a children's science magazine from India. The caption posed a question, "How do people perceive (the theory of) 'evolution' across cultures?" More or less the same way, he found, the wrong way, with false iconography of march of progress and with *sapiens* always on the top.

This time we shook hands.

"Lila," I said.

"Glad to see you again, Lila," he said with a moist and husky voice. "Michael."

■ ■ ■

We spent the night together. In his apartment. Surrounded by his things. Mostly IKEA. I didn't feel like removing my clothes when we went through the process. The more I watched his face, the more I thought about Lucia (and the man who had come to collect her). Michael's skin was more or less like hers, even some of the tumescent moles in the neck area. I didn't stay overnight. Didn't feel like using his shower, gel, his body lotion, his toothpaste. Something within me didn't want to keep staring at his two scuffed suitcases, both blue with four wheels, one in his bedroom and one in the living room near the window, or keep listening to his confessions about having fallen in love with the wrong type, the seventeen-year-old's mother. A second-generation atheist, Michael had ended up marrying a deeply religious churchgoing woman with the family name Kirk. This did not bother me as much as the sound of his pee hitting the toilet bowl, especially the tremendous last few drops. It was a wild opera gone a bit wrong. One more thing. The only genre in his bookshelves was crime, and this fact left me strangely uncomfortable.

Early in the morning I got a call from my editor to do an urgent report for the magazine on an unspeakable disaster in the city's one and only climate lab.

4

3.3 billion years ago there was no ice. Scientists have evidence that our planet was covered by an ocean, that our Earth was a "water world" as the *Guardian* reported this morning. If the findings are confirmed, researchers will be able to refine theories on where and how the first single-celled life emerged.

When the first continents eventually formed remains a mystery. What scientists do know with a high level of certainty, however, is that about half a billion years ago planet Earth was dominated by the supercontinent Gondwana, which lasted into the Jurassic period, about 180 million years ago.

One hundred and eighty million years ago I was not even an idea. I was born after the not-so-innocent onset of Anthropocene, and less than twenty years ago I decided to alter my life, switch gears, by becoming a journalist. I thought the change was going to be small, but as far as human time goes, it turned out to be a seachange.

I had been a geologist. Rather, a student of geology in India. Confession: I was not born into a highly educated family. Nor a scientific family. The reason I applied to the sciences at the university level was my neighbour and high school friend, Gauri.

Gauri. Her name shook me in a nice way when I first heard it. I was drawn to its three enigmatic vowels. We two belonged to the same class and caste, more or less. Our fathers both worked in the railways.

She was the only one in the first-year geology program at the university who really wanted to do geology. Most boys were in the program because they had failed the joint entrance exam to the engineering colleges. Some planned to write that exam (one of the most competitive) the next year, and some were using the department as a stopgap to be able to take the status-enhancing "civil services" exam (each year a thousand are chosen from a million aspirants). There were fewer girls than boys, not unusual, and at least two or three girls told me they were there because it was necessary to obtain a degree before getting married.

Gauri was the only one who made a conscious decision to become a student of deep time.

She did not follow the clothing fashion of the day. I did. She liked listening. I liked talking. Despite a prominent piercing on the right side, she rarely wore a nose ring. Although our aspects looked acutely different from each other, we were nicknamed Siamese Twins. If we had one thing in common with each other (and almost every fresh student at the university) it was our naive desire for peace. We wanted peace in Punjab. Peace in Delhi. Peace in the world.

■ ■ ■

While formulating my article on the disaster at the climate lab, which had to do with Arctic ice, Gauri's face kept surfacing, trying to say something important. Although I denied it then, I heard echoes of her voice. But I had to put her and all associated thought in a parenthesis. My magazine wanted me to rush an in-depth piece on "ice cores" that had been damaged at the lab. Damaged?

"The lost evidence! The evidence of global warming!"

A rare collection had melted away in the most prestigious laboratory in Alberta. Some twenty-five percent of ancient ice samples in the archive room had been lost forever. So much memory, deep-time memory, vanished within a span of a few hours. An older ice scientist told me over the phone that the melted cores had formed puddles on the floor. He could see his own face reflected in "wasted" water. For the first time in his professional life, he had felt like crying.

By the time I handed in the finished copy to my editor (who did a strange about-face and shelved it right away), I was absolutely exhausted. I wasted an entire hour to find out the exact details: there was pressure from the university administration and our otherwise independent-minded boss had caved in. I blamed myself more than I blamed her. Perhaps something crucial was lacking in my hurriedly composed article. What were the melted cores really trying to say to me? I was looking forward to a day off, doing nothing, when my phone rang. I had not saved Michael's number. But I hoped it was not him. I just didn't have the energy to tell him that it would be best to forget each other. I didn't want to use beautiful, insincere words. I didn't want to provide reasons.

■ ■ ■

It was Lucia.

She apologized for her late response. She wanted to meet over tea.

Talking to her on the phone gave me a sudden burst of energy. We planned to meet the next day in the same neighbourhood where we had first encountered each other.

Before my phone rang, I had imagined her calling. I imagined she would invite me to her house, where I would get to see her way of being. She would give me a guided tour of the house. I would end up examining her book collection and knick-knacks and meet her child or children or whatever the situation might be, perhaps say a quick hello to the man who had picked her up. Or at least stand in front of his photograph or photographs in the living room.

I wanted to take a good look at his face. For this to happen as naturally as possible, I had been careful not to bring him up directly during my conversation with Lucia.

From the café table I saw her park her red Volkswagen on the street. She paid for the parking at the automatic machine; she had to punch in the numbers twice. I stood up the moment she entered. She smiled and rushed in my direction. We tried to hold hands, but the angle was awkward. Hers were cold. We were both happy to see each other. She unbuttoned and removed her beige overcoat and placed it carefully on the empty chair. Our table had three chairs, dark varnish on oak wood.

"Sorry we had to rush that day; my husband got a call from the babysitter at home. She had to leave early for some reason, and we had to be home within an hour. My husband works not far from here. His office is only three blocks away."

"No worries at all. Hope your child is all right."

"We have three, a four-year-old, a six-year-old, and a teenager. The younger two are quite attached to the babysitter."

"That day," I said, "I felt like asking you all kinds of questions. So when you left, I had to imagine it all."

"An odd activity it was. I wrote a lot about you as well."

"Please, no need to tell me the details. That would be like breaking the rules!"

"Let me see," she said, moving a bit closer, elbows on table. "Your face looks different today. Forgive me if I am so blunt, for we have *technically* just met. I see some stress."

The waitress arrived with a hyperbolic menu. I ordered herbal tea. Lucia ordered only Perrier water.

"And you," I said. "You look just the same."

I wanted to use the words *happy* and *carefree*. But I restrained myself.

While we were talking Lucia made use of the lid of the Perrier bottle as if it were a small stone calming her down. The yellow lid kept moving and compressing in her hand. Briefly our conversation turned to day jobs. Lucia had studied humanities and German literature at university, but she had never managed to find gainful employment.

Time passed by quickly.

It became clear she, too, had a soft spot for me. We were going to see each other regularly, our body language made it amply clear.

"I don't know about you . . . Shall we eat lunch here?"

Lucia agreed. She asked the waitress if the soup of the day, clam chowder, was any good.

The waitress unapologetically confessed her veganness, but she had heard awesome things about the soup. This little exchange seemed to create a major culinary anxiety within Lucia.

"I am supposed to stay away from dairy. There is a wonderful vegan restaurant close by," she said. "Shall we?"

"Why not?" I said. "May I invite you?" I asked, offering to settle the bill.

She did not object.

While I was trying to recall my PIN number, Lucia's handbag started vibrating. She seemed hesitant to pull out her phone but, seeing me engaged with the waitress, answered in a low voice and moved away for a while.

"It was my husband," she said. "He didn't know I was going to be with you. I told him you are a science journalist. I suggested he persuade you to write a nice article about the new carbon engineering company one of these days."

Before I could ask more details about the company or its carbon engineering, the phone rang again and she had a bit of a chat.

The makeup on her face was so light it almost did not exist. It went well with the colour of her eyes.

"He sounded strange. Needs the car. I asked him to come collect the keys. We can start walking to the restaurant. He will go directly there."

The street was bright, a bit gusty for my liking but bright. Lucia and I walked, lost in our thoughts. The feeling, I assumed, was mutual—we had known each other for eons. A homeless man was pushing a trolley and a few small things fell down. He did not go after them. But soon he stood before a large garbage bin. On the brick wall by the bin someone had planted three fresh bananas, perhaps for him. He picked up the bananas, investigated carefully, smelled them, and placed them back. Slowly he opened the bin and pulled out two or three empty glass bottles and was on the move again, pushing his trolley.

"He looks like Tolstoy," said Lucia.

"Yes, a strange resemblance. Tolstoy in his sixties."

Glass-fronted skyscrapers were reflecting each other; I have no idea when Tolstoy disappeared in one of those mirrors. We stopped at an intersection.

Sometimes the whole world conspires to bring two people together, and sometimes it does whatever it takes to keep them apart. Sometimes people consciously avoid each other, lose sight, change paths, or run away, but keep finding each other again and again.

Lucia spotted a familiar person on the other side, waiting. Waiting patiently. "Oh, there, there!" She waved at a reasonably attractive man. He waved back. We crossed.

■ ■ ■

I did not want to recognize him, but I knew him in a single glance. He could only have been an ex-classmate of mine from back when I was a university student in India. To be correct, he was what had become of him.

Lucia's husband did not seem to place me. If he did, he continued to pretend I was absolutely new to him. As if before that encounter I did not exist at all. He introduced himself with a name I did not associate with the face I recognized.

So I simply told him my complete name and smiled a little extra. Happy that I had not embarrassed myself yet again.

Lucia said, "My new friend would like to do an interview with you."

I had said no such thing.

He was in a hurry.

She grabbed his arm as if to make sure he did not flee. Gently he opened her closed fist and took away the keys.

"Lila is also from India," Lucia informed him in an unusually loud voice.

"Yes, I studied the sciences."

"Which city?" he asked, his Gore-Tex shoes eager to turn in the other direction. He had a very Canadian way about him.

"Chandigarh," I said. "Have you been?"

"No." He moistened the word emphatically. "But I have heard about it."

"Glad to hear."

A yellow Volkswagen Beetle was passing by. It passed. Only then I noticed a Volkswagen Golf tailing it, also yellow. Both the Beetle and the Golf had babies on board.

"Chandigarh," he said, "one of the most beautiful cities ever designed."

"Beautiful," I said. "More so in the past."

5

Perhaps everyone makes an error with a face, the face of the other. When my first proper relationship ended, I would see the face of my beloved in random people and make so many mistakes. It was embarrassing. Once or twice I stopped total strangers in the street thinking they were him. When my mother died, I made the same mistake; it seemed her face left traces on so many members of the living. Perhaps all humans are wired (miswired) to make a serious facial recognition error now and then, especially when it is least expected.

Back home I lay on the bed with my shoes on and kept thinking about the vegan meal with Lucia.

Only toward the end did I mention the object she had lost.

"And I must apologize," I said. "That thing of yours, the thing that brought us together, I forgot to bring it along."

"Funny."

So she had not missed it. The lost object was not as important as I had made it out to be.

"It is a small stone, something you took out of your handbag when we were looking at each other's faces. It never made it back to your yellow handbag. It must have fallen out of your hand as you were leaving."

"No worries... My husband gave it to me a while ago... Just bring it along next time."

I have never been in analysis, otherwise I might have figured out the deep psychological reason why both of us forgot the material cause of our special encounter. In the larger scheme of things the stone has nothing to do with the story I set out to tell, and at the same time it has everything to do with it. That is the thing about *significantly insignificant* details.

■ ■ ■

During the meal she had said that her children were still young, but her neighbour's children had just moved to university, leaving her neighbour feeling like a perturbed fish in a drying lake.

One day, I thought, Lucia would reach that stage in her life and she would feel exactly the same.

When I moved to a university, when I left home, my mother never felt like a fish in a drying lake, because she was already dead. Yes, that was also a possibility. That Lucia would not be alive when her children reached university age.

■ ■ ■

We talked about the sunny setting of the creative writing workshop and the instructor's tweed jackets, dotted socks, somewhat solemn face, and keen interest in certain female students. The young and the very young. Undeniably, he possessed a few good qualities as well. For instance, he rarely stared at you.

Perhaps he stared at his unsuspecting targets like a cheetah. On such occasions he seemed to morph into a wild thing shuffling around with enormous speed; eyes no longer cold and blue, limbs attenuated, pure penetrating claws tearing apart a meal. I will eat some now, the rest later. We talked about it, then Lucia asked me about my manuscript, the difficult novella I was working on.

"Please tell me more than the title."

"Will you be able to keep it confidential?"

"Goes without saying."

My response was an exercise in vagueness. I did not want to reveal that the manuscript had made little advance. Nor the fact that I was well aware of the precise reason for my repeated failure(s). Truth failed to come out. I was shying away from being honest, reluctant to go near the taboo areas. In the novella I was trying to integrate two complicated stories that did not belong together on the page. They did belong tightly together in the real world, but not on the page. One was a major real-world story involving a celebrated scientist—someone I knew only from a distance, a godfather-like figure—and the other was a minor real-world story, something deeply personal, involving me and Gauri and a handful of classmates.

In itself this was not a problem. The problem was that my fear and shame prevented the integration of the stories. On the page a strange rift appeared between them.

Our workshop instructor withheld something crucial from us when he pronounced, "We are the stories we tell."

We are also the stories we choose not to tell. In fact, we are more the stories we don't tell, cannot tell, or will never be able to tell.

■ ■ ■

I lay on the bed with my shoes on, going nearer and nearer Lucia's husband. Perhaps unobjectively wanting him to resemble one of my classmates.

However, I was having difficulties interpreting the way the husband's face had moved on the street. During our brief encounter when Chandigarh erupted on my lips, he emphasized a definitive no. But his metastable face had moved up and down as if he were saying yes, a microexpression impossible to ignore.

I laughed at myself.

India, my inner voice reminded me, is a country of 1.3 billion. People have doppelgängers everywhere, even in countries or on islands where the population is less than a million. Perhaps that movement of his neck was simply a tremor.

■ ■ ■

Explanations come later—sometimes far too late. Or they come with a seeming determination to chisel away at the essence of a past event.

What if there is a name whose face can't be seen?

A face whose name can't be spoken?

What if a face alters when it is being observed?

What if an observer's face alters because it too is under observation?

What if pain forces one to form a phantom memory? While researching an article on cognitive sciences and human memory, I had encountered the story of a woman who was abducted. The room where the victim was abused had a TV. The victim thought the newscaster's face on the screen was the face of the perpetrator.

So much thought crowded my mind, I didn't know how to freeze it or reverse it back to unthought. The street, the busy intersection, kept coming back to me.

During our brief encounter Lucia's husband's eyes had lingered on me. I am able to detect such acts with a high degree of objectivity. Under other circumstances I would have considered it flirtatious, but he had looked quickly away the moment the word *Chandigarh* left my lips.

I reminded myself that all this was rather easy to explain. Sometimes even our microexpressions have multiple explanations. Sometimes what we detect on the face of another is simply a projection. Or a projective inversion.

But I had asked him my main question in Hindi.

Within a blink he had chosen to respond in English.

Even this was easy to explain. Or the fact that his

Indian accent in English had disappeared more or less completely. Such things, I know from experience, are loosely connected to the power and privilege structures in the new world he had moved to.

His gestures, his walk; he was more North American than North Americans.

Was I attracted?

Under different circumstances, if he had not been with Lucia, I would have certainly gone out with him, at least once for a drink or a meal. And now I could not even think of doing anything other than meeting him for a simple interview connected to his work. Because right now I was responsible for Lucia. I had looked at her face from up close.

Perhaps there was no grand logic underpinning the reason that the face of a harmful man from Chandigarh many years ago, a much younger face, a face long forgotten, successfully forgotten, had been triggered by a series of events in Calgary. *Triggered* (a word disliked by some of my friends) was a neutral word for me until that day. That face should have stayed in oblivion as far as I was concerned. Even if I managed to replace the word *triggered* with *awakened*, I would say the same thing.

The face awakened within me belonged to my past, more specifically to a man who dwelled in my past and interfered with my present. Perhaps he was still alive, married with bright-eyed children by now and leading a reasonably happy life somewhere. Perhaps he really was dead, and in that case, I wanted him to remain so. His name was Vikram Jit.

6

Vikram Jit had first appeared in my life when I joined the university. In those days, he kept his hair long in a pony-tail, and like some others, he had a fledgling beard that had never seen scissors. He was reasonably tall by Indian standards. His charismatic brown eyes shone, most of the time, like some divine creature.

He had started the undergraduate classes a few weeks late, something connected to his father's transfer. They had moved from a bigger city, which his dress sense conveyed. By joining late he had missed a few intro lectures, but this had also allowed him to skip the worst kind of ragging, that armed forces–style initiation prevalent in our university (something that always makes me recall the unimaginable photographs of Abu Ghraib). The boys' hostel was infamous when it came to this style of ragging, and rumours made it to the girls' hostel almost every week. Gauri and I shared a sparsely furnished room on the second floor.

By the time he arrived, the ragging had moved to milder forms. One afternoon Gauri and I were sitting by the steps of the Joshi Library, and his seniors sent him toward us with a flower in his right hand. The orders were to present the rose. To one of us. That novice of a man-boy sashayed toward his mission and stood far from us and tried to convey in a low voice that his seniors had made him do it against his wishes and would we accept the flower. Gauri and I looked at each other. He took the delay in our response as a yes, moved a few small steps.

She declined. I melted and took pity on him.

"What is your name?"

"Ruby," he said.

"But that is a nickname."

"Everyone calls me Ruby."

He gave the rose to me. I accepted without a smile.

A loud applause greeted him as he walked back toward his seniors, who triumphantly watched the spectacle they had created. Gauri and I fled the steps of the library, leaving the sad flower behind.

Within a year Vikram Jit, or Ruby, a fast learner, started sending freshmen with red or yellow roses toward newly arrived women students (Amrit, for instance) sitting at various sites on the campus, including the rotunda of a Pakwaan—where one would go to eat channe-bhature and South Indian masala-dosa.

During a field trip to the foothills of the Himalayas to detect the oldest rocks, I noticed Gauri and Vikram Jit having longish conversations. His gaze would linger over me only when Gauri was not there. Ours was the second batch in the department that allowed female students on long-distance field trips. (I still have notes from the trip.) Separate sleeping arrangement for boys and girls, of course. Shared washrooms, strict time allocations. It was the first time I encountered a battalion of cockroaches with fat wriggly legs. A professor taught us how to use all five senses to observe rocks: how to identify a rock by seeing, touching, licking, and smelling after a bit of hammering. How to listen to a landscape. "Sometimes the most silent mountain landscape is the noisiest," he would say. We learned to use a dental drill. How to collect rock samples and from where. "The quality of a field trip depends on the quality of preparation." On the penultimate day two students had disappeared.

Despite best preparations the unforeseen always happens. Despite best intentions the unintended always happens. In the blink of an eye "safe" becomes "unsafe."

Search parties were formed within an hour. But we failed to locate the missing.

While combing the area, we stumbled upon rare birds and a placid sulphur-smelling lake; a classmate who could not take the stress and the heat anymore removed his clothes and dived in. That body, his body, was the first naked male body I saw. He was wearing only the janeau, *the sacred thread.*

Gauri and Vikram Jit stood not far from me. Vikram Jit was trying to brush against her. She raised her palms, covered her eyes.

Nearly thirteen hours later the two students returned. They were limping. Clothes, legs, arms, faces attacked badly by wolves, ears nearly torn apart—the first big shock of my otherwise sheltered life.

■ ■ ■

A week after the field trip Vikram Jit came with a band of boys to the girls' hostel to play Holi, the festival of colours. They had dozens of water balloons and tiny plastic bags, the bags full of bright colours in particulate form.

Some of us were standing downstairs by the entrance. "No wet colours," we shouted, but our voices kept drowning in the uproar.

Confidently, Vikram Jit took a few steps and smeared some of us with dry colours. Then he spotted who he was really after and tried to embrace Gauri as if this was the most natural thing to do, macho Bollywood style.

She resisted and asked if he had consumed bhang, *cannabis* (the edible variety).

"Not even in my dreams," he said.

"Prove it," said the band of boys, and a strange silence ensued.

"Guys." He said something. I don't recall the details. But right after, he started singing, rather half singing, the Bruce Springsteen song "Born in the U.S.A." Using both hands he played his own imaginary guitar along. Electric guitar. Waves of loud intermittent applause kept coming for the next five minutes. Before marching out, he coated the rusty cast-iron hostel gates with colours and ran a finger through it to write a word.

"S-O-R-R-Y."

Months passed by quickly. During those months

I hated the eternal learning of tedious names of fossils and the new equilibrium—it became increasingly clear to everyone in the class that Gauri and Vikram Jit were inseparable. It is all coming back to me now; the tape of memory is rolling on its own.

Because she desired him, and because desire is like that, I too started desiring him. My initial feelings of pity when I saw him getting ragged and disgust when I saw him rag others turned into something different. Strange, now that I think about it. I grew more and more curious about what the two of them did when I was not included. I started envying their relationship, and what seemed to be perfect happiness. Perhaps that is why I was reluctant to share my class notes with him.

He never felt an ounce of embarrassment demanding things. I did. The humiliation of a little folding umbrella forgotten after a fortnight of rain. I felt strange whenever they had a lovers' quarrel. One or the other would compel me to take sides. Twice I took her side, and once his, only to find them patched up and me lonelier than ever.

"What has he done this time?"

"Nothing. Only that he dislikes my family."

"Not again."

"Ruby claims my ma is one of those *devotional mother* types."

"But she is devotional," I said politely.

"Only I am allowed to say that," she said.

I couldn't help laughing. But I stopped right away because her face seemed to suggest it was trying to conceal something from me, something more important. She was wearing a red cardigan with tulip patterns. Our skimpily furnished hostel room was so cold that night.

The warden had prohibited the use of electric heaters to prevent overloading the power grid. It was so cold we changed our plans to paint each other's nails that night, and ended up bundling up and reading out loud from *The Second Sex*, a book we had recently encountered in the library.

Perhaps all this is both a retrospective mistake and a retrospective clarity that emerges from the accumulation of time. Time, I read somewhere, flows in and out like mass or energy, and whatever accumulates (depending on the rate of flow) we call memory. But it must be more complicated than that. Because whenever we say "This is memory—my memory," we refuse to say "This is also my imagination."

In those days few men and women hugged each other. I made it a rule to hug Ruby or Vikram Jit the same way I used to hug Gauri in lieu of hellos and goodbyes. Heart-to-heart contact. Our connection, I must mention, was not as one-sided as I make it sound. Not a straightforward case of misplaced feelings it was. I was in a better situation than a shredding trail of white exhaust that forms behind a flying plane. This is a bad metaphor. Sometimes when I go near him (making circles around his traces deposited in my mind), I get stuck in bad metaphor. I want to come out of metaphor. I don't want to forget good things. Beautiful things that used to make me feel alive.

Nearly everyone in the department knew he skipped classes. Like some minor superman he jumped out of the classroom window right after attendance, which was compulsory. After several jumps he would come to me with a needy face and request my meticulously kept notes so that he could have them photocopied. At the semester exams he always scored higher than me. But never higher than Gauri. I could never understand why he didn't go to her for class notes. She had better handwriting than I did.

■ ■ ■

There was one other mysterious girl-woman in the class, an ultra-silent type. She braided her coconut-oiled hair and dressed as if India had said no to all forms of modernity. She was always eager to share her notes with him.

Our department was a remarkable incubator. First and foremost, an incubator of rumours. One of them, I am able to validate, was as accurate as a gneiss rock. Vikram Jit was taking geology lessons from Dr. G. Dr. G—one of India's brightest scientists—was a well-known name globally. He wore designer clothes and power ties and smoked authentic Cuban cigars. He had discovered graptolite fossils in the Kashmir Himalayas at a very young age, twenty or twenty-one, and published the results in *Nature*. Even outside palaeontology—his area of specialization—he was a mountain of wisdom and knowledge. Once or twice Gauri and I saw Vikram Jit disappear into Dr. G's office. It seemed he had been hand-picked. Vikram Jit rarely bragged about this association. When asked, he said it was his dream to co-author a paper with the great man.

Some of us had laughed then. But it was clear we had laughed because we envied him.

Another boy in the class, a closet poet and a part-time spy (who kept misplacing his compasses), gossiped during a lab experiment that Ruby had a motorcycle more expensive than a Mercedes car.

This boy had a mild crush on me.

"Are you jealous?"

He pulled out a couple of grainy photos from his shirt pocket.

"You are jealous," I said, going through the spy photos.

"No, I am not jealous."

"In that case we are just like a brother and a sister."

"So you don't want to be my girlfriend?"

"You are like a brother to me."

"But you certainly don't know about the international student."

Vikram Jit, he said, rents a small apartment in Sector 42, not for himself, but for an international student, and he visits her every other night. The whole thing sounded so far-fetched I did not even bother sharing it with Gauri. Later I found out that this kind of wild rumour floated around about anyone with a motorcycle.

■ ■ ■

I used to be both happy and unhappy, a ridiculous vibration of mixed emotion, when Vikram Jit crawled toward my places demanding my assiduous notes. More unhappy when he borrowed stuff from the mysterious student whom we called Braids because of the way she kept her hair. She took notes as if she were taking them for him. It didn't take me long to realize that she rarely missed an opportunity to work with him in the labs. However, I never felt jealous of her.

Braids was a minor character in our lives. Her real name was Padma. Gauri and I wondered if Dr. G liked or disliked the girl. One Wednesday Braids used a brand new slide projector to do an overly ambitious presentation. Minutes before the event some of us happened to eavesdrop on a faculty conversation in the corridor. Dr. G was trying to persuade a fellow professor not to ask Padma hard questions.

She always stood third in the exams. Gauri stood first. Vikram Jit second. And fate had nothing to do with it. Nothing in this world of ours is completely predetermined. I can kiss—I kiss—such a design of the world; it awakens me into past, imploring me to give it a different shape. Some parts of my body evaporate, other parts congeal, when I wander through that past. I fail trying to reshape it in absence of disharmony, suffering, and major loss. But I will not fail. I will not fail to tell the story. No matter how it ends.

Padma had the sharp eyes of a peregrine. She nearly lost both of them. One evening in the hostel dining room where we were watching television, our warden's six-year-old boy, influenced by a TV series based on Hindu mythology—Ramayana—shot a toy arrow from a toy bow, oblivious of the consequences. Gauri and I took Padma to emergency. The wound was bad; just looking at her face made me burn. While waiting for her at the hospital, Gauri and I had a long discussion about science and myth. Science was all around us, but so was myth . . . Myths are prettier than science, Gauri's ma would say. But not as pretty as my girl. Mothers are like that. Gauri's ma was a marvellous cook and a deeply pious lady; she kept sacred stones in a small temple at home, worshipped all the incarnations of the goddess Prakriti, and aspired to live according to a harmony principle that respects all life. Prakriti na hile. *So that nature doesn't get perturbed.* (The one problem Gauri and I had with the harmony principle was that it was abused by a section of the more powerful upper castes—our own relatives—to tell the so-called lower castes that the "harmony" of hierarchies must never be perturbed.) The caste system was a wound in our society, an implacable wound that never heals. Gauri told me something I was unaware of. The Vishnu Chakras, the Saligrams, were actually *ammonite* fossils, and the sacred phallic Shivas were *echinoderms* and *cephalopods.*

7

You can rely on a migrant with a scientific background for a non-fancy prose style. A migrant who has dangerously turned off her cellphone for nineteen minutes to seclude herself in order to write.

Perhaps this migrant writer ought to have deleted her incipient thoughts on stories, especially "storytelling about them." Most science stories, I mean the ones narrated in novels, revolve around obstacles faced by a famous scientist. Or they chart the decline and fall of a research star. Often the figure of a scientist is given the role of a hero, a saviour, or a villain.

I run into dedicated practising scientists almost every day and find this kind of presentation severely limited. Imagine calling Lynn Margulis a Rama (god) or a Ravana (demon). Because of such extreme presentations, odd ideas about the sciences float about in the general public, and this makes my job as a journalist increasingly difficult. Real life is messy, entangled, and mostly uncalibrated. Reading a so-called science story always provokes me to question the neat little narratives and the "arc" and other simplifications.

Scientists can be funny, pompous, nervous, mediocre, taciturn, sentimental, dry, full of themselves, nobodies, beautiful, irrational, defensive, inspirational, jargonous, theory validators, theory destroyers, bitter, dull, weird, compassionate, blackmailers, wicked, brilliant, workaholics, patriarchal, ambitious, vain, sex-obsessed, contradictory, pattern makers, compartmentalized, compartmentalizers, envious, hyperconnected, egoistic, sterilized, dreamers, uncertain, dispensable, manipulative, monkish, rivals, irresponsible, collectors of good data, collectors of bad data, full of desires, cautious, grand, happy, wise, careful, question makers, boring, hopeful, decent, single-minded, peripatetic, two-faced, characters, performers, socially awkward, or gracious.

There is a Calvin Klein or a Prada type and there is a cotton-kurta-with-blue-jeans type and there is a holes-in-the-socks type. In other words what one is dealing with is ordinary mortals and not gods or monsters. So many of their stories are left out. Left out even when the story is told by someone to whom it happened.

Why?

If only I understood all the mysterious *whys*. But this I know—we design our nights and days according to weather reports and remain glued to our smartphones as if they were the most essential organs of our bodies (even as we tweet the most anti-science sentiments). When there is a health issue almost all of us go to a doctor before going to a religious shrine. We don't trust politicians, banks, law firms, big media, big business, Facebook, the military, or art dealers, but even if we claim we don't believe in science, our everydayness suggests otherwise. Of course some of us don't have a rigorous training in the sciences, but we all have a story. Stories similar to or different from the ones scientists tell or assume about their discipline. But there exists a different class of stories, the ones we don't hear, assume, or tell. The kind of story not even the scientists tell—or not fully anyway.

■ ■ ■

What I really want to process is Gauri. She was all set to become a remarkable scientist. I had anticipated (like everyone else in the class) something monumental from her, but that was not to be. Perhaps what I am consumed with is our inevitable friendship; I had imagined it blossoming in unexpected ways over a lifetime, but that was not to be. Perhaps I want to unravel the essential strands of the *relationship* between Gauri and Vikram Jit. Perhaps I want to process myself, all the stuff still opaque to me. Perhaps I just want to liberate myself from her story because I am afraid the same thing might happen to me or someone else.

Since I left Chandigarh (*fled* is not the right word) I have been back once. To take notes on the state of science in contemporary India. This was also the first phase of a series of articles I planned to write on the impact of humans on Earth and climate systems.

The day after my arrival the mercury crossed 50°C in Chandigarh. Middle-class neighbourhoods sounded like an adagio of air conditioners. The local population had more than doubled during my absence. The city was spraying the asphalt roads with water to make sure they did not melt, and the white painted zebra crossings resembled natural-born Pollocks.

At my old university department I met a skinny ghost of a figure, one year my junior. She is an assistant professor now, set to become the queen of Indian geology. I wonder what Gauri would make of this.

Amrit hugged me mechanically and we walked briefly through the labs and halls and corridors again, the concrete building where I had spent four years of my life in a daze. Everything looked different. On the walls—more names. Gauri's name absent from each and every list of honours. Amrit's and Padma's names everywhere. This didn't come as a surprise. But I was pleasantly surprised to find out that nearly half of the current faculty members happened to be women.

"How come?"

"How come?"

"Nearly half . . . a mini-revolution."

"Most are daughters of professors or powerful

fathers," she said. "Have you forgotten?"

"It is all coming back to me."

"Normally these posts would have gone to the sons—"

"But now they have opened up—"

"For the daughters as well."

"What are you doing in 50°C?" I asked. "You seem to be the only one in today."

She stared at the dusty computer screen for a long time.

"Someone has to do the work."

"You were always the best," I said.

"Second best!" she said.

"Where is Padma these days?" I asked. "Remember Padma from my class?"

"*Braids* is a big name in vertebrate palaeontology these days," she said. "She works at that second-best place for geology in our country!"

We talked about Gauri. Only in passing. It was clear she no longer thought about her. Perhaps the whole department had dropped her in the well of oblivion.

Our conversation was cut short by a power failure. She was sweating, beads as large as red berries. Our necks and foreheads grew moist—almost supersaturated. She was dressed in a white T-shirt and thick blue jeans, her cheeks glistened. She kept smiling faintly, so as not to bring about a shift in the mood. "Do you have children?" she asked.

"No," I said, a bit startled. She asked again—perhaps she did not hear my no—and I gave her the same one-word answer and no reason or apology. After a brief pause Amrit's face transformed, and she nearly broke down recalling briefly the year she was pregnant. She'd had to hide her pregnancy from her male colleagues in the department. It had been incredibly stressful.

We talked about the stresses of a changing climate and the alarming rate at which the groundwater level was receding in Punjab, in all of North India. Her most quotable lines: "Mother Earth is showing a mirror to modern-day kings" and "Most of these new disasters are *unnatural* disasters." I wanted to ask several questions, especially the one my magazine is always keen on: What would you do if this were the last day on Earth?

But I ended up asking about her child.

She had four or five shelves full of books. Messily arranged, as if an homage to the goddess of entropy. Ironically, it was in that office I encountered a strange and familiar book: *The Creation Myths of the Gond Tribe*. Remarkable cover. The visual on the cover: a *night tree* painted by a contemporary Gond artist. Amrit wanted to give it to me as a gift. She said, "Take it for your child." Only then she realized making a mistake. "Take it anyways." Foolishly, I refused to accept and wiped my forehead with a tissue. "Take it. Gauri gave it to me as a gift." Really?

"One must never give away what one received as a gift," I said.

"But she was your friend."

I could not tell her. I could not tell her that Gauri, too, had received the book as a gift from some distant relative . . .

I recall that early morning scene in our girls' hostel. There was a faint smell of yesterday's sweat in the air. Gauri said she liked the book, but the relative was a *character*. "He exaggerates when he says I am losing my culture—he doesn't know that culture is not fixed; it never was." Gauri smiled enigmatically. "I belong to my culture more than him! You see I find it difficult to say no! I couldn't say no to his gift!" . . .

Before the assistant professor and I parted, the power returned, and she and I drank two bottles of Aquafina water. She read her favourite myth aloud to me, and every bone in my body was speechless like a happy child:

"Billions of years ago there was nothing but oceans in the world. Water was the beginning and the end was water. Bara-Deo stood akimbo on a lotus leaf feeling bored. Bara-Deo took a deep breath and rubbed Bara-Deo's chest and from body sweat shaped a crow. 'Bring me clay,' Bara-Deo said to the crow urgently. The crow flew liquid distances, but nowhere clay was in sight. The crow landed on top of a tiny island to catch a wink of sleep. The island was the claw of Crab. Crab secretly disclosed to the crow where all the clay had gone: 'The clay is diminishing as Earthworm is eating it slowly.' 'Help me,' begged the crow. Crab nodded and pulled Earthworm out of the damp dwelling and squeezed its neck. Earthworm spat out a cascade of particles of clay. The crow beaked the particles and flew back to Bara-Deo, where Spider was weaving a giant web. On the web, placed just above the waters, Bara-Deo shaped the continents and Earth's creatures from clay. But. There was one big problem. There were no trees. So Bara-Deo made trees."

■ ■ ■

I was lying on the bed with my shoes on thinking about all this when a ping sound announced an email. My phone rang almost at the same time. It was the older scientist from the climate lab, the one who had grown emotional looking at his face reflected in Arctic puddles. He wanted to share two or three "significant enough things." His voice sounded less anxious.

The magazine publisher had stalled my article. I did not tell him.

He apologized for not giving me access to his lab earlier.

"No worries," I responded in a Calgary-esque way, thanking him for his willingness to shed more light on the accident.

"Come to the lab now?"

"I will hop on the train in fifteen minutes."

"Bring along your polar gear."

"Will do."

Can one see the future by looking at the past? Not just recent past but deep past? The astonishing field called palaeoclimatology allows scientists to pull off such an incredible trick.

He was waiting in a green sweatshirt outside the

concrete building. Despite a strong urge to observe him from a distance, I took a few steps toward him. His wrinkled face was remarkable. The closer I got, the more I felt that he was carrying some strange disturbance within. As if a silent convulsion was moving through most of his inner selves. Slow like the deep Earth itself.

"Hello."

"Hello."

The main zone of his climate lab was the ice archive, which was kept at -36°C. If I were a layperson, the zone might have appeared as a storage place for fish without the smell. He must have struggled with himself. Something made him change his mind about giving me access. He treated me to a guided tour. This was crucial for an improved version of my article, an opportunity to convince my boss to run the story.

The opening lines matured. *A transient smile, almost a regret, appeared on his undefeated face. I wondered if "Holocene scientists" ever experienced such emotional states. What would it take to reverse some of his regret?*

Inside the archive one felt in the company of literal ghosts. Those neatly labelled cylinders hid within them traces of the climate that existed tens of thousands of years ago; they concealed within them bubbles of methane and carbon dioxide and oxygen—fossilized air—and bands of ash from old forest fires and volcanic eruptions, even radiation from nuclear weapon testing.

"What on Earth is an ice core?" my father had asked during a recent phone conversation. At times he ends up asking just the right kinds of questions from the point of view of my prospective readers. I gave my curious eighty-year-old father the short version. To study past climates, scientists drill a glacier or an ice sheet metre by metre. One can go as deep as 3.2 kilometres. A core drilled in Antarctica in 2004 yielded eight-hundred-thousand-year-old ice. Some call it three-kilometre-long time travel. One returns "home" with evidence. Someday the scientists might return home with five-million-year-old ice. In a nutshell *ice cores* are drilled cylinders of ice (a metre long, about ten centimetres in diameter). A collection of such elegant cores is no different from some of the most important fossils that enlighten us with past climate information. During my undergraduate days in India a male professor used an odd metaphor. Think of an ice core as a Shivling, *Shiva's erection*, he had said. I didn't tell my father that.

The climate lab scientist told me that he explains ice cores to Canadian undergrads using the analogy of tree rings. An archived ice core cylinder reveals annual bands of ice, like a giant Douglas fir tree reveals rings.

I was allowed to touch the polarized light apparatus and one actual ice core.

Spontaneously I removed my gloves and held a core for a while.

An old poorly preserved memory flickered. I didn't want to go near but she flickered.

Gauri's eyes had lit up during our second field trip in the Himalayas. Her face suggested both curiosity and a predicament. By this time we knew the principle of superposition, we understood gradualism and catastrophism, we no longer believed like early geologists that mountains form because Earth shrivels like an apple. Geology, we were told, was about "past," but this past was on a different scale. For us Earth scientists it was safe to ignore humans and their grand activities. The opening and closing of oceans and formation of mountains had little connection with the construction or destruction of human houses and monuments, nor with agriculture, battles and wars, slavery, colonialism, not even with the railways or the extraction and burning of coal. We were blissfully unaware that in only a matter of years, geology itself would face a major disciplinary crisis. Deeply embedded habits of thought and assumptions would go haywire. The ignored "human" could no longer be ignored because, collectively, the merely biological "human" had acquired a geological agency. Of course we knew about the carbon cycle, but we still didn't have the "Earth systems" approach. Most meaningful questions revolved around "a change in stratigraphy." One of our major tasks was to learn to *read* rocks, to become close readers of rocks. Gauri and I had to learn to read testimonies of non-human witnesses, varieties of dead non-life locked in layers of rocks. Some witnesses were completely flat, others were soft bodied, almost three-dimensional. While taking photos of Triassic limestone, I heard her say av'shesh, the North Indian word for a *trace* or *fossil*, and soon enough she freed her hand and rubbed two fingers on tiny egg-shaped formations (as small as a millimetre), and she had passed her fingers over the embedded shells as well. At that moment she was simply one with Mother Earth, her hand feeling all the traces of time accumulated inside that material. That mere mortal was in total contact with something extraordinary and yet so absolutely ordinary. That soft, slow passing of two whorled fingers on Triassic limestone was irreversibly wonderful.

■ ■ ■

Suddenly I feared a severe injury.

Frostbite.

I was shivering.

Outside the archive, in a much warmer part of the climate lab, the older scientist brought us two cups of black coffee.

Small wrinkles around his eyes. I kept observing them as he started a prelude to his testimonial. His voice was wrinkled as well, and largely resembled the voice of a character, a ship captain, in the Netflix crime series Michael screened for me for five minutes and kept referring to when I was at his place.

"Canada has a big reputation outside of Canada. Not many know that only a few years ago many research labs were shut down here. Climate scientists were muzzled, censored, or fired across the country; instructions were sent to stations up north to simply dump the ancient Arctic ice cores in parking lots."

"May I record this?"

He nodded. The delicate skin on his lips looked more than chapped.

"Was this when the Conservative Party was in power?"

"During the right-wing regime we lived in a constant state of fear; a scientist was ordered to get permission from the senior-most cabinet minister before he could speak to reporters about a flood that happened thirteen thousand years ago. We were afraid of instant dismissals. A routine call from media outlets or curious students could fill us with dread. It used to take eleven government employees and over fifty emails to decide how to respond to a journalist's request about info on regional snowfall patterns.

"Some good things happened as well. During the nine-year-long Harper regime our laboratory went out of its way to save the Arctic ice cores. There was no way we were going to allow Ottawa to orphan them in parking lots."

I let him speak.

"Not a single cylinder got dumped. We did the right thing then. We adopted the ice core collection from the Ice Research Lab in Ottawa. We trucked the collection 3,500 kilometres across the country to the safety of a caring lab in Alberta. But now . . ."

"But now?"

"We the saviours, so to speak, have ourselves destroyed what was saved. You already know some of the most sensational aspects of our loss: an ice core from the Penny Ice Cap on Baffin Island lost nearly twenty-two thousand years of history, while a core from Mount Logan lost sixteen thousand years.

"Trust is hard to gain, easy to lose. We are trying to minimize the blame. Our key argument against transparency is that climate deniers will misinterpret the 'accident' and spread malicious messages."

I paused. Longer than necessary.

He filled the gap and explained his earlier reluctance to give me access to the archive. Shyness. Lack of trust. During our phone conversation and a brief Skype chat, he saw me as no different from a run-of-the-mill reporter. He must have googled me after the Skype; he must have been reasonably impressed.

I chose not to follow up on this subject. I didn't allow that off-the-cuff phrase to change the basic register and polite tone of our conversation. The puddles were more important than me.

"What made the ice puddle? You said a part of the storage room felt like a steam bath?"

"Official reason: equipment malfunction. The heat-removing motor in the archive room malfunctioned. Instead of pumping heat out, it started doing exactly the reverse and the room grew intensely hot very, very rapidly, a step change. Fire alarms turned on. If the motor had not turned extremely hot, no fire alarms would have sounded and we would have lost the entire ice collection."

"So it was an accident?"

"Off the record—the archive had no backup cooling system. The samples had been rushed to a new facility, against a warning delivered by experts, so that the top administrators could milk the buzzword *An-thro-POE-cene*. *An-thro-PAW-cene*. Many high officials received bonuses, etc."

My interviewee was silent for a while.

"Do you smoke?" he asked.

"I gave up long ago. But can I ask you something personal?"

"Maybe."

"Why did you shave off your beard?"

He smiled.

"My six-year-old grandson wanted to kiss me on the cheeks. So I let it go."

"So I let it go," I repeated and smiled just like him.

I could have spent more time with him—he wanted me to—but my thoughts were occupied by someone else, someone trying to persuade me to make it a part of the difficult novella I was composing.

When I moved out of Chandigarh to Canada, I did not miss the people left behind. More than people, I missed language and landscape and animals and objects. I missed monsoony verandas and trains and rickshaws and fabrics and designs and jacarandas and neem and banyan and guava trees, and things, some of them only tenuously associated with the people one was supposed to miss. I would grow nostalgic for a canvas tent pitched near the Silurian and Devonian rocks in the Himalayas. I missed Gauri a lot. She, too, had become a thing.

■ ■ ■

Gauri's death was an accident. We were a group of sixteen returning on a night train from fieldwork in the Shivalik foothills.

Fourteen of us were in our seats. Two seats were empty. Gauri and Vikram Jit stood near the doors of the train car. We could not see them from where we sat. When I went to use the washroom, I happened to glance at them briefly. One door was open. A homeless woman with mental health issues was sitting on the floor near the closed door, not paying attention to movement or stillness or the world around her, certainly not to the two students standing near the open door. She was making chapatis. I can still see her. Although there was no dough, no rolling pin, no griddle, no fire, the woman in shalwar kameez was going through all the motions of making chapatis. No idea why I recall this ember of a detail more than anything else. Vikram Jit's brown shoes on the verge of losing their colour. His expensive blue jeans blatantly well-worn. Gauri's hair was fluttering in the wind. One of her hands clutched tightly on the thick bar and the other to her backpack.

I returned to my seat, to that noise; the whole class was singing a priceless eight-hundred-year-old song, clapping. A portable cassette player was our accompaniment. On full blast. Laal meri paat / Dama dam mast qalandar / Dama dam mast qalandar / Char chirag tere balan hamesha / Panj'van mein baalan aayi / *Your shrine o' qalandar / Always lit with four lamps / I have come to light the fifth one.*

Five or six or seven or eight minutes later someone pulled on the emergency brake.

The train came to a complete stop.

We heard Vikram Jit's voice.

I can still hear it, a faded version of his loud, nervous voice.

Gauri was found, with the help of torchlights, by the tracks a kilometre or two behind, smeared by mud and red rock flour. Dead. Right after, Vikram Jit got the madwoman arrested by the railway police.

"She pushed Gauri down."

8

The police found nothing unusual about Vikram Jit. But a Panjab University geology professor who had accompanied us went through the contents of Gauri's backpack, which was also on the tracks, and recovered a fossil. It belonged to the geology department's palaeontology museum.

Most of us agreed. This unusual fossil was not the one Gauri had collected. In fact there was no chance in the world of finding that fossil where we had been wandering.

I remember *wandering* on that trip. We walked along a limpid brook with an excess of eddies and vortices. We adjusted each other's hair; her hands smelled of rocks. Briefly we talked about men. Men who gave us fevers or talked about us as if we were mere frost on window glass. Nothing unusual—a routine conversation. We ate Amul cheese, cucumber, and tomato sandwiches. We saved a couple of apples for later, as if no one were going to die. Gauri told me a story about a coal mine in Bengal. Her anthropologist friend's father was a manager at the infamous mine. She was going to persuade him to organize a visit. Her anthro friend was a living encyclopaedia of juicy facts, and she passed the tidbits on to me. Things like "Before the British came, not a whole lot of people burned coal in India. Before colonialism some people even made ornaments out of coal."

The clouds lowered and darkened and the thunder-storm came suddenly, so we made a sudden decision. We threw away our geological hammers. With the metal gone, we were safe from lightning.

One could always depend on her alertness. I was re-luctant to let go of my hammer, but she raised her voice: Pagalpun na kar.

Just before the storm she had started sharing a recent conversation she'd had with our senior-most lab techni-cian. What did she want to tell me? It is important now; it didn't seem important then. The story slipped us by. I never found out.

I blame the storm.

I blame myself. For I didn't want to talk about *indoor laboratories* that day.

Reluctantly, I blame Gauri. She told stories so unhurriedly.

Later she had stopped abruptly and picked up a geomet-rically delightful piece of wet quartz. She cupped the quartz close to her ear like a conch shell, trying to listen to its voice. I don't want to sound metaphysical, but she wanted some-thing from that quartz, something more than geology.

When I think about Gauri, I think about her death. And when I think about her death, I intuitively know it was not an accident. What I know nothing about is how that fish fossil got in her backpack.

■ ■ ■

I was not the only one who suspected Vikram Jit or Ruby. But soon after, nearly a month later, almost the entire class, me included, moved on to a different explanation.

Often the stories we transmit and the stories we tell ourselves get revised. Sometimes it takes eons or centuries, sometimes a few hours. We don't expect them to get revised so quickly in so short a period of time, but the fact of the matter is that they do get revised, even revisions get revised, and the role time plays in all this appears so puny in the end.

Gauri's story found itself revised briefly after her death. I rely on the word *aftermath*. In the aftermath of her death, something equally significant occurred, something no one saw coming. Something that stirred the calm sediments and the bottom-feeders all over again. Something I don't want to go near, not even in the dark runnels of memory.

9

I saw Lucia next at our bimonthly fiction workshop. The instructor recapped. Golden rule number one: "Quickness on the page." Golden rule number two: "Speed."

What if the narrator prefers self-reflexiveness and privileges a meditative voice? I asked myself. Or wants to slowly process feelings and emotions and textures of everydayness? Or what if the main focus of a story is the carbon cycle, which takes a million years to complete? What if the narrator wants to go beyond the usual interior monologues to something epochal—say, a character's epochal stream of consciousness?

The simple algorithm of his narrative tricks carries a built-in bias, I thought, and I raised my hand. "Some of us are not against movement. I want things to move, I want thought to move. But to me, slowness is a quality as important as quickness."

The instructor rubbed his nose with the tip of his finger. "Good point," he said, racing through his notes, and he vectored off. In the group setting Lucia's and my interaction was reduced to a mere seven minutes, but we managed to have tea afterward at Tim Hortons, where, among other things, we agreed to get together the next day to do some urban fieldwork for a moderately complex assignment: *place* and *character*.

Next day at the appointed hour I could not locate her at the entrance of the art gallery, the site of our assignment. The weather was a strange, nebulous thing all of a sudden, a clothing and emotional confusion. I made sure my phone was on, bought a ticket, and walked in to take in the temporary exhibition. Pieces by Albrecht Dürer and Max Beckmann and a few other important works from Europe were passing through the city. Because of the oil boom, Calgary could afford to bring in great works of art.

It did not take me long to spot her. Even before I entered the main hall, I saw Lucia's profile; she was sitting in front of a Max Beckmann triptych, although at that point in time I did not know the title of the triptych. Instead of rushing toward her and saying hello, instead of trying to locate the exact title of what she was so taken by, I found my steps retreating a bit. I searched for a spot in the hall where I could observe her clearly until she turned her neck backward on her own or walked away. I didn't want to compete with what absorbed her attention.

The guard, in full blue uniform, kept her eyes fixed on the teenager who was going around and around the hall without looking at the paintings. I, on the other hand, was not bored; I was simply observing a friend, absorbing her as efficiently as a solar panel absorbs the sun. I was obviously engaged in something odd, something no one else in the hall was doing, and to reassure the guard I took out a pen and a little journal and wrote a word down every now and then.

Our instructor had asked us to write about objects (and their transient relationship with a curious character) in a public setting. I had no idea where other workshop participants went or whether they went alone or in pairs, but Lucia and I had chosen to do our fieldwork together. Just the previous day, while having a quick tea with Lucia at the Tim Hortons, I had proposed checking out the new natural history museum, but she, without providing a reason, said it would make her feel uncomfortable. She had proposed the German exhibition then.

Now she was completely absorbed. From where I stood, I could see other museum visitors go past her, some glued to their phones, others saying sorry to Lucia if they temporarily blocked her view. The microemotions on faces around me were indiscernible; it was a pity. Two or three times I heard the sirens outside, but this had little effect on her.

There, taking notes, avoiding the guard's curious movements, I glanced at Dürer's charcoal sketches. The one that spoke to me was an edgy portrait of his aging mother. She looked like a woman from India.

Someone new walked into the hall. He started circumambulating the room just like the teenager before him, but seemed to pay attention to all the big and small Beckmanns as if plotting to take copious notes.

Perhaps he was from some other creative writing workshop.

So many workshops had sprung up in the city, right after the oil boom. For some strange reason most workshops had science- or engineering-sounding names— Filling Station, Black Whole, Gravity's Bow, Carbon Positive, Free Fall. Ours was an acronym, TAOS Writers. TAOS stood for tar and oil sands, not my favourite acronym. Despite the names, most participants had little scientific training, and their writing was anything but. Other than me and a lab technician at the Foothills hospital, no one showed much interest in the sciences (and decolonization), although a man based in rural Alberta aspired to write science fiction like Philip K. Dick.

I move back to the main thread of my thought. Despite a proliferation of writing groups, no one had managed to tackle what I thought were the essential stories of new Calgary. For instance, no one had managed to write a book or books about Gatsby-style figures who had acquired tar sand dollars all of a sudden. A journalist friend of mine, based in India, had written *The Beautiful and the Damned* about Gatsby-style figures in new India, rolling in oil and metal and mining and polyester and coal rupees, but no such literary creation happened in Calgary or Edmonton or Fort McMurray, for that matter. Once in a while one saw a short story or a poem with words like *bitumen* in it. But really. Most workshops, I was informed by a colleague at my magazine, were preparing "ghostwriters" for "can-do" oilmen to compose memoirs. I would kill myself if someone ever asked me to become a ghostwriter.

The previous day during our tea, Lucia had asked me again about the details of my project. The workshop instructor wanted the first drafts of our novellas within five weeks. I did not know how to summarize Gauri's story for her benefit. It was the only story I felt necessary. But to tell her story I had to tell so many others, including the story of Professor G, and I didn't know how to bring him to Gauri's story organically. So all I told Lucia in response was that it was about geology and climate change. Climate change emotions.

She told me about her climate anxieties then, and her guilt. Children. Future. Waste. Plastic. Farmed chickens and bones. Diaper waste generated by her own children. She told me she went through depressions. She was on medication and that was why she looked so happy all the time.

I didn't know how to subtly ask if the depression was connected to climate change, so I asked her directly.

"Maybe," she said.

I have a feeling she put on filters. Perhaps she was not comfortable with the fact that everything, or huge chunks of that everything, eluded her as well. But she did share something. While she was doing so, I listened carefully as if the rest of my life depended on whatever little she was going to share.

Lucia was around seventeen when she moved from Germany to Canada. Her German father had chosen a popular Spanish name for her. She was going to be called Pia or Lucia; the latter name had won in the end. She had been back to Germany only once.

Lucia was now taking no notes sitting in front of the Max Beckmann triptych. She had on a long beige overcoat; she must have simply forgotten to remove it. Her yellow gloves rested peacefully on the wooden surface beside her. Half an hour had passed; she was still completely unaware of my presence or the glowering guard being replaced by another.

I sat down on the settee near the other wall; this way I could still see her and detect the exact moment of separation from the triptych. I picked up the large-format book that accompanied the exhibition and flipped through text and reproductions, some in colour, some in black and white.

The one funny or sort of funny thing she had told me was how she had met the man who later became her husband. Both, students at Uni Calgary, lived in rented rooms off campus in a quiet neighbourhood. Although he was in a basement room in the bungalow across from hers, they remained completely unaware of each other's existence until the day three or four vehicles with sirens (lights flashing) stopped in front of his house.

From the patio of her prairie house she heard the foreign student talk to the uniformed men (not cops, no squad cars, not firemen, no ambulances, not emergency medical staff).

She found out later the real reason for confusion. The student had grown up in India calling mice *rats* as well. So when he saw a mouse in the basement he had called the city right away. To keep the city rat-free all residents of Calgary (in fact all residents of the province of Alberta) are supposed to report it immediately if they spot one, especially a Norwegian rat.

The uniformed men showed the student neatly labelled albums full of photographs of the rats they were after. He had pointed toward the photos of mice then, much to their relief. And yet they had cordoned off four or five houses and sprayed chemicals wherever they thought it was necessary.

While she was telling me all this, I studied her hair and face. She did not squeeze her nose to convey a trace memory of disgust. She was having a lot of fun narrating the story. Disgust must vanish if it becomes desire, I thought.

When I asked about her own relationship with rats, she paused longer than necessary. My question made her uncomfortable. Perhaps this explained her physically distant relationship with the natural history museum as well.

Two or three lines formed on her forehead. I didn't persist. She told me on her own, but I felt she was editing it all. All the fun she was having, the carefree abandon, melted in the air. She said she had heard fairy tales and fables from her parents, and although she had written an essay on Art Spiegelman's *Maus*, she did not know how to tell the difference between a mouse and a rat either, and those coloured pictures the uniformed men left behind were useful.

My new friend recalled a wartime "rat story" she had heard (in German) as an adolescent. A little boy posts himself by a little patch outside the rubble of his destroyed house; he says he is keeping vigil, guarding his little brother. Because rats might eat him. A passerby hears all this, understands the sad situation, and informs the boy that he should stop keeping the vigil at night and go inside the house and get some rest because rats sleep at night.

She was standing in front of Max Beckmann's *Falling Man* (1950) now. She moved a few steps, planting herself in between *The Night* (1918) and *Family Picture* (1920). I kept observing her and what she was observing. *The Night* made me think of Picasso's *Guernica* (1937). It seemed *Night* and *Guernica* had been created by co-painters rather than an individual Picasso or a Beckmann. It seemed *Guernica* inspired *Night*—although temporally speaking this was impossible. It seemed the spell would last until closing time. No noise could break it. The spell was finally broken a bit by the creation of sudden silence in the hall. The last ones to leave were an old woman in comfy clothes and a girl with two mute button symbol tattoos by her ears. By this time the guard, my skin colour, had left as well, as if I could be trusted completely. Lucia moved, checked her cellphone, turned.

It was a delight to witness her big simulated smile.

"Didn't want to disturb."

"Oh! I was waiting," she said. "Thought you were never coming."

"It is bad manners to interrupt a writer lost in deep thought."

"I am disturbable!"

"Sometimes?"

"Always."

Both of us were famished, so we walked to the museum café. All the surfaces at the café were alive because of the café's choice to play jazz and blues. Trumpet. Saxophone. Cello. The young woman who gave us the menus made an eye contact only with Lucia.

We drank two bottles of mineral water right away. After ordering the daily special—fungi-margherita pizza —I took the stairs down to the restroom and washed my hands. It was a last-minute decision to eat pizza with my hands. The restroom had a naked bulb on the wall. The oval mirror beneath the bulb had a small (but infinitely long) crack in the middle; it made me resemble a runaway or that woman in *Carnival* by Max Beckmann. I was looking older than my biological age. Skin completely dry. I had to dig out Gauri's miniature hand mirror from my backpack to take a proper look at my face.

During my brief absence a small family had occupied a table not far from ours. The mother, armed with a heavy-duty digital camera, was taking endless photos of the baby. Beads of sweat gleamed on the woman's brow. Her husband seemed to be playing with a little plastic doll. The couple had another child, a brown-haired daughter, about five years old, and she kept wandering, now and then asking the owner, "Do you know how to fly?"

Salad was part of the daily special. We didn't have to wait long. Several times Lucia's thoughts turned to Max Beckmann and the beginning of a new phase in his life. I ate pizza slices with my hands. Wonder what she thought about this.

"Which Beckmann were you most drawn to?" I asked.

"Let me think," she said. "Of all the works here I would say *Dream—Chinese Fireworks*."

"Why?"

"Because nothing in the painting is exactly what it seems."

The little girl, something profound brewing in her mind, came running to our table. "I give flying lessons."

Both of us made eye contact with her parents. The mother smiled. "Okay," I said. The girl repeated "okay" three or four times and started moving most of the chairs unsteadily to the side, creating a mini-mountain, but really a long passage to act as pretend "runway." The owner didn't seem to mind either.

"Watch me." From one end she started running, flapping in her hands two red napkins, as fast as she could. Breathless, she returned to our table and "whispered" loudly something important in Lucia's ear. "Now you know!" Excellent, I said. She spoke very fast. "If you manage to flap these napkins fast enough, you don't need to run at all. You start flying from wherever you are standing. Or sitting. Understand?"

Her mother came to our table, kissed the child, and took her away.

"Up and up and up you go," the child continued.

The owner brought us honey pistachio baklava and decaffeinated coffee; the conversation with the girl had made me feel a bit vulnerable.

Lucia paid for both of us. She would not allow me to. We walked to a used bookstore in East Village. It shared a wall with a refugee shelter. But a very old man with brittle hair, standing outside, told us that it was closed and would not reopen for three more days.

"It is a pity," said Lucia.

The old man repeated, "It is a pity," finding it difficult to stop.

We walked back to the Centre Street LRT train station the way we started, and soon we were on different tracks. Before parting, our handshake had transformed spontaneously into a hug. She said, "I call you." We had no idea that it would be a long time before our paths crossed again.

On the train I felt a mild ache in all my muscles. We had walked and stopped and walked for over six hours. Surrounded by new but anxious faces in the carriage, my thoughts raced inward. And I knew it was time. I must never let such episodes make me doubt my decision regarding children, I said to myself. My unwavering decision not to have one.

And yet. How I yearned to be like Lucia, to have someone in my life, to be able to say that I cannot live without this or that person. But the fact of the matter is that all these years I have not felt like that toward anyone.

I thought about Lucia, especially the seventy minutes or so she spent looking at the Max Beckmann triptych.

The changing expressions of her face, the flow and discontinuities of her thought, were still floating within me. I was becoming more aware of my ambiguous feelings. For a moment I myself didn't know if I was pursuing Lucia's man or Lucia. Because nothing in the painting is exactly what it seems, she had said.

One must never lose sight of one's main focus, what one sets out to do, as Gauri used to say.

The train picked up speed between Crowfoot and Tuscany. I looked out of the window. Everything was getting ready for the dark.

10

Today I did nothing. Only zoomed in and zoomed out of the following sayings in geology:

The past is the key to the present.
The present is the key to the past.
The past is the key to the future.
The future is the key to the past.

II

Now I know a few things about imperfections and limitations, my limitations. Now I understand how one is
able to be both open and closed at the same time. Both
unshy and repressed at the same time. So much about my
relationships with men (and women) was opaque to me
then. I thought and felt that I was a good interpreter of
people and an objective reader of myself, someone who
had figured out the basic laws, the organizing principles.
All along I felt I saw through (and kind of sniffed at)
the fictions humans lived by; I would look at my mother
and father, relatives, and acquaintances and it would not
take me long to figure that most of them were hoping
to finally live their lives exactly the way someone else
had imagined. This was also the essence of my bond with
Gauri. The unspoken assumption that we had somehow
managed to resist such "collective fiction systems," that
we had stepped out. Now I know better. There is no "out."

There is no out, but a new type of feeling has replaced
the old type. Now I feel as if there are too many unrelated
things placed in front of me. They are placed too close to

me and I am supposed to read them effortlessly, the way one reads text printed on a sheet of paper. My eyes are wide open, but all I can visualize are molecules of ink and pulp and fibres and filaments and binders that make up that white rectangle of paper. The more I try to zoom out, the more I zoom in.

■ ■ ■

Lucia must have felt very close to me because she shared not just the topic of her "fiction" project, but also its origins. I had no idea that she too was working on a crime story.

"Perhaps I don't want to know," I said.

Something within me is convinced that Lucia developed more trust in me the moment I said that. *Because you don't want to know, I am going to tell you. Once you know, you cannot unknow. Not being able to unknow will have its consequences. Because you cannot unknow, you will try to know more and more.*

"The project has to do with a longish visit to Europe last year," said Lucia, right after taking our selfie. Hard to forget that gleam in her eyes. The gleam and the smile didn't represent her inner state, and the more she spoke, the clearer this became. "Business class. Everything paid for."

"Wow."

"We all accompanied my husband to a small fairy-tale town in north Germany."

"How come?"

"My husband received an invitation from the Institute for Advanced Study to spend four months as a senior fellow in the sciences. The town is located near several research labs, so my husband was interested. Cutting-edge, he likes to say. The institute provided furnished apartments to fellows with families."

"How lucky!"

"We found it funny. I was returning to Germany because I married an Indian."

"An Indo-Canadian," I said, "with a wonderful name."

"Amitabh Ghosh," she said. "He likes it."

"Fantastic name indeed," I said. "Nice ring to it."

"Really?" she said.

"It suits you as well," I said.

"Really?" she said. "I changed my family name."

I responded with a gesture, as if using words was risky.

"Anyways," she continued, "a week before the flight I typed *Germany* in Google, thinking I would find out how the local media were reporting the recent arrival of migrants from Syria. I was expecting semi-good or semi-bad news about the upcoming elections and the fate of Angela Merkel. But none of these showed up as the top news items.

"There were long reports, even Sunday sections, about a nurse who had killed over three hundred people in a hospital."

"In Germany?"

"Deutschland."

It was clear the way Lucia began sharing (the kernel of her own crime novella) that she had not shared it with anyone else, not even the instructor. She searched for words, not her usual style. I also got the sense that she had already anticipated such a chat before stepping out of her suburban home that morning. All along it was she who was in control of the situation. If she felt unready in some way, she would have awkwardly (or otherwise) turned the conversation elsewhere. She had chosen me as her sole audience. I listened. Tried to make meaning.

"How did they catch her?"

Lucia was quiet.

"The nurse?" I said.

"The reports did not make it very clear. But they eventually caught him. His photos dirty the internet now. *Shame.* I cannot forget the nurse's face. He always followed the same method. Induce a heart attack in a patient in the intensive care unit. Then try to revive them, succeeding nearly half of the time. Whenever he was on a shift more patients would suffer from a heart attack. He would even get awards for saving more lives than other nurses.

"During our flight to Hamburg I thought perhaps all this was happening in what was previously known as East Germany. But when we arrived at the Institute for Advanced Study in the small town of Delmenhorst near Bremen and Oldenburg, we found out that the hospital in question, St. Joseph's, shared a wall with the institute campus.

"The first night after putting the children to bed, I found it difficult to sleep. Even a harmless piece of information provided by one of the wonderful research managers at the institute started affecting me. The cheerfully bald manager said, 'If you ever get locked out you must go to the hospital for a spare key.'

"The male nurse no longer worked at the hospital; the reports on Google had appeared all of a sudden because of his trial. There was no need to be afraid. The fact is I was not afraid. *Anxious* is a more appropriate word.

"During the day my husband would drive to Bremerhaven to be with climate scientists at the Alfred Wegener Institute and I would walk with the children to the city. On the way we would see the hospital on our left. Beautiful brick expressionism architecture, no longer in fashion. Past the hospital there was a cemetery. I was told the police were still collecting evidence, more and more bodies were being removed from the sprawling tree-lined cemetery and transferred to the forensic lab. Some said the number of people the nurse had played God with was beyond five hundred. Several had been cremated and that evidence was lost forever.

"My husband is an amiable man. He works hard and whatever little time he has he tries to make me happy. He senses right away when I am feeling low. To cheer me up, he took me to Elbphilharmonie an hour or so away in Hamburg, but in the dark concert hall, listening to Bach and Górecki and Hindemith, all I could think of were the doctors and other medical workers who worked with the male nurse. Those who knew, sort of knew, suspected, sort of suspected, but did nothing. Before the nurse started work at the hospital in Delmenhorst, he worked at a bigger hospital in Oldenburg, and the doctors and nurses, according to the trial reports, did nothing. Well, that is not true; the administration at the Oldenburg hospital ended his job there with a strong letter of recommendation for possible hiring at some other hospital, and that hospital happened to be next door to the fellow apartment allotted to us.

"The three months we spent there I was unable to enjoy the weekly—late evening—public presentations delivered by my husband's colleagues. Most of them, like my husband, were collaborating with teams at Germany's most prestigious climate research laboratory—the Alfred Wegener Institute—in Bremerhaven. Of all the presentations, I remember just three. Not the actual experiments, but a patchwork of facts. I learned how important a role technology plays on Earth. 'If all modern-day technology is magically removed, human population might as well drop to around eleven million.' Someone was working on whale songs. I learned that millions of years ago the ancestors of whales lived on land; they walked like raccoons, before evolution sent them back to the oceans. I learned that up until 2.4 billion years ago there was no oxygen in air. Earth is 4.5 billion years old. Life on Earth is 3.5 or 3 billion years old. I told my kids. They don't really know the difference between a million and a billion. Neither do I. We were unable to go visit the house where

I was born; I was unable to teach German to my *kinder*. I skipped driving them to Worpswede, a nearby village where the poet Rilke spent a chunk of time. The only thing we managed was a rushed tour of the migration museum in Bremerhaven. Something happened 2.4 billion years ago. The oxygen level shot up. I started smoking again. One night I got drunk and walked with my husband's colleagues to the hospital to say hello to a certain ward. It became a routine. Every weekend I would get drunk and ask someone to accompany me to the hospital. Or we would simply try to peek inside. Night and day I read more and more local and national papers. Magazines like *Der Spiegel* covered the story in considerable detail. I consulted the city archives. The nurse was married with children and he used to shop in the same Lidl supermarket on Hannah-Arendt Strasse where we would get our groceries. Same Rossmann drugstore, same Aldi.

"When we returned to Calgary, I thought the hospital would disappear from my mind on its own. Exactly the opposite happened. The nurse shot up in my dreams just like the oxygen level in air had shot up 2.4 billion years ago.

"In one dream, or nightmare, he, wearing one earring, was seated comfortably by a large glass window in the corner. On the marble tabletop, a half-eaten croissant and an espresso. The newspaper he was reading had a large grainy black-and-white photo on the cover— patients from all over the world, wearing medical masks, trying to find a way into a hospital. The little espresso cup shook mildly in my hand; my hand separated and accidentally killed a silverfish.

"One morning I started writing down the dream. And a week later I joined the writing workshop."

■ ■ ■

Listening to her my body shook in a strange way. Vibrations I call "metastability." She was no longer telling me what she was telling me, but her words remained hung between her lips and my ears. I had no idea how Lucia was going to shape that real-world story down as a work of fiction, a story at once major and public. I can only speak about my failure to integrate the public and private crime stories from my own life. Gauri and Vikram Jit's story remains minor compared to the major story that I have not even partially processed so far, despite the dreams.

■ ■ ■

"Do you have a title for your novella?" I asked Lucia.

"Not yet."

"I have an excellent title."

"Really? What should I call it?"

"*Silverfish.*"

Her face tried to smile. She gave me no clear clue about the value of my suggestion.

"This seems like a story of the night. Story of nocturnal

walks. Story of complex characters unable to mingle with the night. Why not begin with your walk to the hospital with your husband's colleagues?" I said.

"Am I in your novella?" she asked.

"Am I in yours?" I answered.

12

We migrants are like snowflakes (or clay particles); each one comes packed with a unique story. A dangerous story. But that is not the main thing. Above all we are filled with hope. Even our stoicism and cynicism are corrupted by hope. Despite this, at times we ourselves do not know the exact reason why certain things haunt us.

I arrived in Montreal, Canada, when Trudeau (senior) was no longer the prime minister. On day two, I climbed up the congealed mountain to see the beautiful Catholic cross. I saw Trudeau (senior) walking down the same crunchy trail. I had to pinch my shaking forearm when he waved and smiled at me. I recall saying to myself that it was different from being in India where the prime ministers and ex–prime ministers are cordoned off from the masses by layers of security.

Not every encounter on the street was pleasant right after arrival—the intercontinental move stressed my belly and throat—but I cannot forget the ebullient faces of a little boy and a little girl, dizygotic twins, standing outside their red-stone house, who said a sweet

"Mademoiselle, je t'aime" to me. I did not know what the phrase meant. I did not know any French.

I was so ignorant about certain things. I did not know that Cree was a language. Unaware that in the Cree language, the nouns do not have gender, for they are categorized as animate or inanimate. Not always easy to predict. A rock, for instance, is animate.

In Cree, colours are verbs. Not "black" or "yellow" or "red" or "blue." But "being in the state of appearing blue." Colours are verbs in our language and not nouns of white supremacy, a Cree elder told me.

You look like a peace-loving woman, the elder told me, but migrants don't have a good reputation here. The European migrants who came to Canada conducted genocides. Europeans who went to Asia and Africa and the Americas, as you know, conducted genocides there. Human, non-human, and environmental genocides. As violence goes, migrants can be extremely violent and they take more than their fair share of resources and land. You cannot even begin talking about climate change if you do not begin talking about stuff like this, the Cree elder told me.

■ ■ ■

If I had stayed on in India would I be classified, along with 1.3 billion people, as a non-migrant? I never bothered to ask such questions while living and breathing in the country of my birth. Recent ancient DNA studies bring evidence that everyone in India—like everyone in the rest of the world—is a migrant and everyone is "impure," a mongrel. Not a bad thing. *Homo sapiens* are all migrants, all mixtures of populations that were themselves mixtures of mixtures, and so it turns out we are related to each other in wonderfully diverse ways. We are related even if we recount the story otherwise. Ancient DNA studies are questioning the neat little narratives told by the right and by the left and by bleeding-heart liberals. Ancient DNA analysis is already de-creating stories streamed by those who hate too much or love too much. To be able to date the great mixing and migration events of the past, and to be certain about it, is no mean achievement. Careful! Several pet theories of archaeologists, linguists, and historians have already collapsed; others are being reborn. Careful! Ancient DNA is allowing the dead, actually the ears of the dead, to tell their stories themselves—as precisely as possible! To investigate the Indus Valley Civilization, population geneticists got DNA out of a tiny ear bone from the more than four-thousand-year-old skeleton of a buried woman! One of the most humbling conclusions of ancient DNA analysis is that there is no such thing as "blood and soil" or "place and people," not in India, not in Europe, not anywhere. Hybridity, movement, change, all the way. Of course. I am listening.

■ ■ ■

When my move to Canada was still fresh, I followed the developments at *home* as if I were still there. More than that. I even marked someone. By following the oscillations in that individual's life, I thought it would be possible to get an approximate idea of how my life might have turned out if I had not changed continents. But this marked person moved as well, in an antipodal direction, and married someone who owns a sizable collection of perfumes and nine gas stations in New Zealand or Fiji. We lost some contact, before losing all contact.

Canada provided me with a fresh experience every day. New eyes, if not the new world. Helpful for someone trying to forget that they have forgotten a few things.

■ ■ ■

One recurring image in the chains of unease in my dreams and nightmares is Gauri's body by the tracks. Her face surrounded by rocks. Someone kept saying, Where is her pillow? Where is her pillow? Where is her pillow?

■ ■ ■

During the return journey the moon was half-full or full, which is the same thing; that night it was the same thing. During the return journey Vikram Jit injured his leg. The part-time spy in my class told us that Ruby fell on the tracks during the commotion that followed the death. I noticed blood on Ruby's pants and a slight limp in his walk after the officials disappeared with Gauri's body. The limp lasted a few days; it didn't seem permanent. During the return journey I held on to Gauri's suitcase in the train. No idea why my inner voice didn't force me to return the scuffed suitcase to her mother right after arrival. She found out about it from other classmates and came to my hostel room a few days later.

Strange, now that I think about it, the cops did not ask me for the suitcase either.

Before handing it to her mother, I dug through the contents and decided to keep a kameez and a cardigan of hers in my wardrobe for a few days. The clothes are still with me. Also the hand mirror.

"Are all her things still in there?" Gauri's mother had asked.

"Yes."

■ ■ ■

One day I wore that kameez of hers. No one in the department seemed to notice that it belonged to Gauri. They only wanted other people to notice what they had on. Back in the hostel I took a cold shower. I stood under water for almost half an hour. The kameez clung to my skin tighter and tighter as if a second skin. An uneasy feeling fell on me. I don't know the word for when someone feels they are being unfair to science. She was not around, but I could not help but fantasize that she was, that she was something more than a voice inside me.

Someone knocked.

I turned off the shower.

Someone knocked again.

"Who is it?"

A male voice.

"I am Gauri's uncle."

"How did you get in here?"

"Don't worry, Gauri's mother is also with me."

"How can I help you, Auntie-ji?"

"Lila bay'ta," she said, "we have come to collect Gauri's kameez."

"Thing is," I said, "it is gone."

"Where?" demanded the uncle. "We are waiting."

I had intended to give the kameez back to Gauri's mother, but the presence of her uncle made me change my mind. He did most of the talking. The only thing that separated us was a slim bathroom door; the wet kameez was in my hands.

"Come out," he said. "We are waiting."

"It is too late."

"Why is it late?"

"Because I lost it."

"But you wore it this morning. Everyone in the class noticed. A boy from your class called us at home."

"The skinny boy who always wears blue and writes poetry? Did he phone you?"

"We are waiting."

"Auntie, I was going to bring the kameez to your place on my own. How could I keep it with me? It got mixed up with my things. When I wore it this morning,

I simply didn't realize the mistake. After returning from the department, I changed and washed the kameez and put it out to dry on the balcony railing. I am sorry. It is no longer there. Some fifteen minutes ago a Shimla monkey jumped onto my balcony and took it away."

It surprised me. The two of them were not mad at me. What followed was a long silence. All three of us were grieving in our own unique ways, and that was the meaning of that silence. Gauri was not going to come back, and that was also the meaning of that silence.

Gauri's mother said something soft then and recited a prayer in Pahari language. The only word I understood means a blessing.

■ ■ ■

Lucia had provoked me in a good way. She belonged to some old school of oral storytellers. Listening to her, especially her crime story, provoked me to find a way to integrate the prickly strands of the minor story with the major story in my novella. The major involves a man who was less a man and more a duke or a prince of science. If I know something about him it is via others. What others would tell me, and what they continued to tell me until they stopped, not because there was nothing more to tell, but because of a simple realization that certain things would always remain hidden.

By the time the story broke out in international media in 1989 (that history-making year of the Berlin

Wall, Tiananmen Square, and the ozone hole), it was already two years old. Panjab University's research star, Professor G, the one who had a nose for discovering fossils, not just the run-of-the-mill variety but index fossils that mark geological time, had committed the biggest scientific deception in the twentieth century.

He had published over four hundred papers (with around 113 co-authors) and seven books. His "work" of nearly twenty-five years had in effect "polluted" vast areas in palaeontology.

Whenever I try to slip this real story into a pub conversation, people find the whole structure and plot unreal, and I start doubting myself. The distinguished research star buys a Moroccan fossil from a shop in Paris and claims he dug it up in the Himalayas. He steals an educational fossil from a lab in Wales and reports that he located it in the Himalayas. He moves a fragile fish fossil from China and makes a diagram depicting its discovery in the Himalayas.

Professor G was first exposed at an international conference on geology in Calgary in 1987. It feels like a long time ago, but it is not even a geological blink. The prince of Indian geology was himself in attendance, sitting in the audience (the front row) when an Australian researcher presented a paper laved with high detail on the so-called discoveries.

G stood up. Denied everything. The prince of Himalayan geology raised his voice and threatened to sue the Australian.

Some 250 people in the room prevented the distinguished scientist from physically attacking the whistle-blower.

Many more months passed before the story broke properly in the international media. The foreign whistle-blower had gone public after receiving death threats from Dr. G. Because G was exposed globally, Indian media had to follow. Never before had the press in India done this kind of reporting on ammonites and graptolites and conodonts. Even people with no scientific training found themselves talking about fossils. I recall those days with great clarity, the precise moment in my life when a real interest in science journalism was invoked.

The whistle-blower published many of his findings in *Nature* in an article called "The Case of the Peripatetic Fossils." The prince of Indian geology got a fair chance to respond. In the letter he wrote to *Nature* and in newspaper interviews he took refuge in arguments like "jealous colleagues," "racism," and "the Australian whistle-blower, Dr. T, is a Pakistani agent." One alternative fact after another.

What intrigues me about this case is what others did, or did not do, or what was done to them.

G's powerful connections at the university, including the vice-chancellor, kept everyone confused for years on end. Dr. G's lab technician at the university, the one who was going to reveal the hidden stuff to the inquiry commission, was murdered.

13

I am looking at the essential reading list prepared by our workshop instructor. One highly recommended book is a Swedish crime story by the author Henning Mankell. The instructor distributed two photocopied pages from the middle of the book and spent twenty minutes discussing a scene that involves a police officer who feels bad that the young woman he wants to help is actually afraid of him. She runs away from him and tries to hide in a burning field of corn.

Not because of anything he did, but because of his uniform.

I don't know if the family members of the murdered lab assistant got any help from the police. Police do not work for people "who do not matter."

Professor G lacked faith in direct action. He did not kill the lab assistant directly, according to all accounts. Someone got paid a heavy sum to carry out a smooth hit-and-run accident.

Gauri's death was also labelled an accident.

I have no proper proof. Proof that's considered reliable, that can stand firmly on ground. But no official questioned Vikram Jit. No one in power positions suspected the good guy. People believed his version. He got the madwoman arrested. When the railway cops handcuffed her, she was still at the same spot where I had seen her making imaginary chapatis. She was standing, no longer sitting, still at the exact same spot. She was muttering gibberish, eyes popped open, her face looking as if she had seen something horrific. There is no way she could have run toward the two of them, no way she could have pushed Gauri down from the moving train.

I could not share my thoughts with the police.

Gauri's parents were devastated. At the same time they were relieved to find out that she had not thrown herself down on the tracks. Relieved that she had not committed suicide like the international student whose body had been found on the tracks just outside Chandigarh on the night of Leonid showers earlier that year.

And me? Perhaps a part of me was subconsciously happy that she was no longer, and no longer with the person I desired.

How I hate myself now for desiring the same person I suspected.

I could not even suspect him properly then.

■ ■ ■

Lucia called. We discussed a writing assignment.

Toward the end she mentioned that all of a sudden, her husband was curious about her work.

"Early in the morning he asked about all the novella projects at the workshop!"

"What did you tell him?"

"Most projects are speculative fiction," she said, almost a giggle.

"Did he ask more?"

"I didn't tell him much about your project."

"How did you characterize my work?"

"Lila, it seems to me, is making lots of things at once; at times it seems she is making science fiction, at times I get the impression that science fiction is her turkey and fantasy literature is her stuffing."

"He was okay with that?"

"He made a bad joke about cranberries."

■ ■ ■

Michael had left three or four messages. The last message was really long and ended with the words *ill-mannered*. It was necessary to phone him back. He was unhappy, but his mood improved and we had a sort of conversation. I told him as clearly as possible that we should not see each other anymore. I told him about an upcoming conference. Despite my lack of interest, he offered to drive me toward Burgess Shale, the site of the conference in the Canadian Rockies. This was a nice gesture because

I do not have a car. Obviously, he was having problems absorbing what I had just told him directly. When I declined and repeated what I had already told him, he got back at me indirectly. Conferences are nice places to *meet people*, he said in an ill-mannered tone that meant *sleep around*, and I terminated the call a bit abruptly.

Yes, conferences are nice places to meet people, but such dramas often take place in novels and in film. In real life less than one percent of people go through such motions, not that they don't have desires.

Michael had found one of the books I was looking for when we first encountered each other. *Creation Myths of the Gond Tribe*. It is a 1949 hardbound edition, he said like a romantic on the phone. A Miami Public Library discard. Literally untouched. Come to the shop at the very least, he said. My response, a single word: "No."

"Give me your address," he said. "I will have it couriered."

The only reason I gave him my address was because I really wanted to give the book to Lucia as a gift.

14

Sometimes I feel sayings like "The past is the key to the present" or "The present is the key to the past" may not solve human problems. More and more I think in terms of past-in-present and present-in-past, and this has been helpful.

I was not the only one who somewhat suspected Vikram Jit or Ruby. But nearly a month after Gauri's "accident," the entire class, me included, moved on to a different explanation.

Vikram Jit killed himself.

He was declared dead.

We heard about it all many hours before that short article in the middle of the *Tribune*. Pesticide poison. Froth from mouth.

I cried. The whole class cried.

A private cremation was held. Death by suicide makes people closest to the family say and do some irregular things. The family had found a way to protect itself from such irregularities.

For us at the university, the suicide was validation.

A validation of love. Life without Gauri made no sense and Vikram Jit had joined her in death.

■ ■ ■

The boys' hostel and the girls' hostel organized a joint memorial three nights later. Psychologists have known for a while now that memorial events are helpful to begin properly the long work of mourning.

■ ■ ■

These days I drive less and less. I gave up my car some dozen years ago. I use rental vehicles only when absolutely necessary. This has not been easy. For many essential things, like trips to supermarkets, I still rely on the generosity of friends who own cars, and this makes me feel in the middle of the night nothing less than hypocritical.

I drove to the conference listening to Gould's rendition of Bach on CBC Radio. Near Lake Louise I stopped briefly for gas (resisted the temptation to buy Coke and chips) and soon after I almost ran into animals. Plural. Three brown bears, a family, one of them a bit grizzled. When my breath returned, I tried to think about the long-dead "animals"—the Burgess Shale fossils. Although not so well known in popular culture, this 1909 discovery of creeper-crawlers and its revised analysis shed more light on the history of life than all the knowledge we have so far on dinosaurs and their asteroid-caused mass extinction.

The conference organizers could not have found a better site for conversations on Earth and climate systems. I was especially looking forward to two presentations. One on the French ice heritage project, and the other on Greenland by Annabel Sotto, the new director of the climate lab in my city, about work done at the prestigious Alfred Wegener Institute in Germany. The older scientist I'd interviewed at the climate lab wanted me to meet her. He was more than favourably impressed by her work on fossil DNA.

I arrived a couple of hours late. The ten-minute coffee break had just started. The main hall was noisy. Little groups had formed. Some were using this opportunity to network ferociously. One scarf-clad man with intense bushy eyebrows was a real magnet. One woman (wheeling a laptop bag) was avoiding another woman (wheeling a suitcase). One was eating baby carrots. One was going around asking for a smoke. One Calvin Klein–clad D.H. Lawrence face lifted his left leg up in the air. A tiny piece of gravel had stuck to the sole of his shoe. The tip of his index finger sheared it away. At this point I felt a hand on my shoulder. The older scientist was happy to see me. "You must meet her." He pointed toward the woman with the laptop bag.

Seeing us approaching, Annabel Sotto waved at the ice scientist and turned and walked away with her bag. Clearly a bit nervous before her presentation.

Conferences are strange sites for gathering stories. I feel overwhelmed and lost. My usual method is to follow the work of one or two scientists closely. I am more interested in their everyday lives, even their intimate lives. Do their relationships break down because of climate change? Do they encourage their children to migrate to places that may fare better in the near future?

We had to wait until the end of Annabel's talk on Greenland for a proper introduction. She was more relaxed now. She held both my hands and said, "I have heard so much about you."

The older scientist stood with us, smiling. It seemed they had known each other for a long time. She had also accompanied him to collect ice core samples from Kenya, where he was originally from.

"Let's meet at the café later, around seven," she said. "We will be able to chat better then."

During lunch I saw the two of them catching up. I didn't want to disturb them. So I sat down all by myself.

For a while I was only interested in the curried cauliflower soup. Slowly I was intrigued by sounds wafting from a group at a faraway table, all of them from Alberta. "The Black guy, the Black guy." This was followed by nervous group laughter. The small group seemed to be in complete agreement, trying to say something "nice" or offensive about Dr. Richard Kimeu—the older ice scientist—but I did not get to figure out the exact details.

A perfect gym-casted body passed by, clearly not interested in my company.

It did not come as a surprise when I spotted Amitabh Ghosh in the same dining room; his name and event were listed in the program. He was part of another large group seated not far from my table. I waved. He returned a vanishing acknowledgement. Perhaps that is why I decided to move to his table. There was no empty chair, so I took mine along and people at the table created space for me. However, we could not have a proper conversation, it was simply too noisy. An insufferable Swedish scientist kept cracking strange jokes about the Danes. The Danes speak with bread in their mouth, that kind of stuff, utter rubbish. Ghosh was rather silent throughout lunch; once in a while a smile fluttered on his lips. I could tell why Lucia had fallen for him.

■ ■ ■

His presentation was in a couple of hours, right after the one on boreal forest fires. I did some photocopying. The near-noiseless state-of-the-art machine was on the second floor. On the wall across from the photocopier hung two framed Burgess Shale fossils, *Opabinia* and *Anomalocaris*.

Outside the window powdery snow had just started to fall. Curtained by thick layers of clouds, the Cambrian fossil–carrying Mount Stephen was completely invisible now. Only Emerald Lake was detectable. The trail around the lake was marked by reluctant traces of human footsteps.

A deer-like creature appeared out of nowhere. Nimble and beautiful with antlers and big eyes.

I put on my red sports jacket and hurried down the carpeted stairs. The revolving door was out of order, yellow taped. I used the emergency exit. Outside was a sudden, welcome brush with peace as I traced the freshly made path. Snow fell in a relaxed manner as there was no wind to drift it into doing something dramatic. I didn't brush off the accumulating particles from my face. Pebbles, stones, rocks, enigmatic five-hundred-million-year-old worms with soft tissues preserved, and us. Outside I was a forager. Keeping my distance, I followed the antlers.

Our eyes met only once.

Startle, followed by stasis and incomprehension.

■ ■ ■

Cold, crisp air had calmed and comforted me and I was in a good mood. The animal's face and gaze kept flickering within me like something uncanny on the edge of apparent symbiosis. I was back at the conference centre well within time to attend the 3:00 PM session.

Amitabh Ghosh's packed presentation bowled me over completely. I witnessed most of it standing at the back as there were no empty chairs left in the hall. I felt he had the best content at the conference. He spoke about the technology he and his associates—mostly white and male; the company was headed by a US-trained Harvard University–based expert—were developing to remove large quantities of CO_2 from the atmosphere and convert it into a value-added product. Up until this point I thought his research was no different from what many others were trying to do: decarbonization. But fifteen to twenty minutes into the presentation, he switched gears and asked honest and courageous questions about something considered taboo, strongly taboo within certain scientific circles. He spoke about the need for a massive climate engineering experiment, for which the technology already existed and was remarkably cheap: spraying controlled amounts of sulphuric acid in the upper layers of the atmosphere to reflect sunlight and thereby reduce global warming. "Stratospheric particle injection," he called it. He confessed that many still thought of this kind of intervention by a nasty chemical as something forbidden, but he begged to differ from the detractors; this was the best way he knew of to save millions of people at risk, especially in less developed parts of the world. It would save humans and their cities, save forests and other species too. Crop yields would go up. A win-win situation. The results of this kind of geoengineering would be clear almost instantaneously.

■ ■ ■

After the talk I planned a scramble but ended up circling the lake instead. It was hard to form an opinion. I did not know whose side I was on. He said he loved nature, he loved skiing. He had the best possible solution to a *wicked* problem. "To save nature we must do more than simply manage nature. We must manage how we manage nature."

He had managed to both seduce and scare me. We are confronted with a problem far more severe than our best mathematical models and empirical data reveal, he said as he projected the rate of change of CO_2 plots on the screen. "Scientists got climate change so wrong—they kept lowballing the threat." In a sombre voice, Ghosh had quoted a journalist who called his company's proposition "a bad idea whose time has come."

Where will all the sulphur come from? "From the tar sand towns like Fort Mac just seven hours north of Calgary." Two or three in the audience had asked difficult questions about severe health risks, possible flooding, droughts, desertification, and how this style of geoengineering might disturb the monsoon in India and China, triggering "monsoon wars." Someone called the proposition insane. Someone was concerned about termination shock and rapid warming if the injections were stopped prematurely, a recipe for mass extermination. Someone from Asia called him a US agent. Someone did not like "injection" as a metaphor. "It would do nothing to prevent 'poisoning of oceans' and only encourage people to use more coal, and the skies will be no longer blue," they said. Of course, the presenter responded, the skies will turn white and hazy during day, but we will beautify our planetary sunsets. The skies are already dirty yellow in many parts of the world, and at night we see not a single star.

I knew I was going to write a stunning article.

Sometimes the only way I process my thoughts is via writing. I do not know what I know until I write.

■ ■ ■

She had said around seven.

When she didn't show up at Le Café, our meeting place, I had a vortex-like feeling that I was either extremely late or extremely early. I waited for fifteen or twenty minutes, flipping through newspapers. I could have called her room using the hotel phone or sent an email. But that would have ruined the effect. Five more minutes passed by. I walked all the way to her room.

She took a bit of time to come to the door.

"Oh, you!"

"If you are busy, we could do this some other time."

"Sorry, I forgot."

"No worries."

"The Twitter trolls," she said by way of an explanation. "I was upset again."

Annabel was not wearing a bra under her slim blue T-shirt. We were still hovering by the door when the phone she was holding rang. She did not wait for the second ring. Most likely an urgent call from a cable TV news anchor to gather sound bites about her colleague who had just won some genius award sponsored by Bill Gates. She put it on pause for a second but lost the connection.

"We can do the interview now. Will you be brief?"

"I will wait for you at the café."

"Come in . . . We could . . ." are the words I heard. Perhaps she said something else.

The phone rang again. She was a busy woman. She answered and then gestured at me to enter the room. She muted the phone for a split second. "Help yourself to wine in the fridge," she said.

I felt embarrassed for invading her privacy, but I also felt that we two would get along really well. She had made a split-second decision to let me in, and I had also made a split-second decision to step in. She was a busy woman. She had granted me the interview. Did she want something in exchange? Obviously she wanted me to write a good story about a good person. Was there something more? What else did she want from me? Perhaps she was too busy and eccentric to pay attention to such things. I felt safe entering the room. When four or five top male scientists had invited me to their hotel rooms in the past, like her, I had either found excuses or muttered a firm *No*.

Excellent light inside. There were two dwarfish wineglasses on the table next to a half-read book on the brilliant scientist of Gaia and symbiosis: Lynn Margulis. The wineglasses were shiny and empty, but they looked used.

I removed a bottle of Sauvignon Blanc from the refrigerator (mostly coffee beans, olives, cheese, strawberries). I took two new glasses from the cupboard.

Annabel carried out her phone chat, clearly longer than expected, in the bedroom. The door was partially shut; nothing was visible.

I heard a whisper.

It was clear. There was someone else in the bedroom.

She returned and initiated conversation. We were both making more eye contact than usual. Her face was youthful, a well-preserved *energy-momentum tensor* of strange and familiar emotions. Still no mention of the person in the bedroom. A child, perhaps, or her partner. At the conference the only person I had seen her hanging out with—Dr. Kimeu. He seemed very fond of her. The two of them not only looked like a couple but operated like a couple. I instinctively knew something was going on between them. They definitely belonged to the one percent who do hook up at conferences.

Someone turned on the tap in the bathroom.

At this point, Annabel knew that I knew there was someone in the bedroom. Yet not a word from her.

She was in a hurry, but she was extremely polite with me, generous. I did not want to begin the interview with Twitter trolls, nor with a Big Question, so I began with a recently surfaced childhood memory. Back home in Chandigarh, whenever a book would fall from my mother's hand, she would pick it up and bring it in gentle contact with her brow and ask for forgiveness. I was eight or nine when I noticed a bunch of books fall from her trembling hands, and this time she asked for forgiveness from one book only. Ma told me it was not necessary to request forgiveness from each and every book because all the books that fell from her hand were interconnected and equally important. "They breathe the same air."

I shared with Annabel what was bothering me. On several side tables in lounges at the conference, I encountered some badly written, badly argued books authored by climate deniers. Some non-participant had strategically planted the books to poison the site. One book began with a factual statement of a sentence: "The Arctic has warmed three times faster than Earth since 1971." The next sentence went completely feral and counterfactual: "Pure myth-making . . . Greatest hoax ever."

Annabel nodded and nodded and nodded and shared with me the sheer dread she used to go through during her younger years when a paid climate denier interrupted her presentations. "Much to my surprise nearly half of the interrupters happened to be women," she said. "One came to a presentation on purpose to attack me. This woman was not one of those friendly skeptics you encounter now and then, the one who listens when you explain. 'You are a liar,' she said, angry that the university had not kicked me out. 'You are a mouthpiece of climate hysteria!' It was clear she had memorized a bunch of lines. 'Your bogeyman fear is far below the accuracy of measurement! One of the basic principles of physics is that you cannot measure a micro-organism with a foot ruler!' What should I do? I thought. I let her talk, and she grew angrier and angrier. Soon the audience members began intervening. One tried to explain the carbon cycle. I didn't have to do anything. She called me a 'piece of shit' and sent a barrage of hate emails afterwards.

"When I was young, I wrongly believed that if only

people knew all the facts about climate change, they would see through everything.

"When I was young, I used to love answering questions like 'How do you know this or that? You were not there.' Now I am very careful who I am talking to.

"There is yet another type. This one doesn't perform anger in public spaces. He milks doubt and uncertainty and openness in science. He publishes a flawed paper in a non-peer-reviewed open-access journal, or submits a 'paper' based on fake data sets to a prestigious journal, and while the work is being reviewed—say, by *Science* or *Nature*—he claims on his website that it has already been accepted for publication. He abuses the reputation of the journal to widely circulate his so-called conclusions and withdraws the paper before it is rejected.

"Regarding the books you encountered on the side tables," said Annabel with a poker face, "one of my grad students, without informing the conference organizers, has already discarded them."

"Recycling bin?"

She took a deep breath.

Both of us picked up the wineglasses at the same time.

"What is the most astonishing thing for you working in the sciences?" I asked my favourite question.

"This ability," she said, "this ability to switch from human time scale to geological time scale within a split second and talk about three billion years ago as if it were yesterday's rain."

"Why did you join the sciences?"

"Because as a teenage girl I was trying to process a single line once uttered by my maternal grandfather: *Human civilization depends on geological consent.*"

"Does this still surprise you?" I asked.

"What surprises me now is that collectively we humans, too, have become a geological force. The more I think about it, the more I am not surprised. All along we remained obedient to a dangerously stupid concept propounded by Charles Lyell that human action was insignificant in the history of the Earth. Of course Lyell can't be blamed for what followed him. In the sciences whosoever challenged the concept with empirical work was ignored because of the global economic interests of the West."

"Are we talking about a disciplinary crisis?"

"Disciplinary crisis, yes. Even civilizational crisis. For geology. For history. For all other disciplines, yes. Even for the human."

"For journalists—no!"

She smiled.

"Is it fair to say that most Western geologists carried on with the business of geology as if they were executives in a cigarette company?"

She paused.

"But," she said, "don't quote me on that. I have a lot to learn about the history of Earth sciences, and I know it is more complex than that. I would say we geologists are Janus-faced. We develop knowledge and at the same time exploit it in ways that also make us agents of destruction."

"Who is your biggest inspiration?"

"Gary Vermeij of Uni California," she said. "An extraordinary palaeobiologist. He makes us see what we fail to see. His publications come without diagrams or images. Because he happens to be blind."

The wine was sweeter than my taste buds expected. I was feeling relaxed. I could have stopped there. But. Some rapid movement occurred in the bathroom. She did not bat an eyelid.

We switched to Annabel's work, the recent presentation. She grew more animated, used lots of gestures while responding to a question about the microbial analysis of ancient ice core sections from Greenland and Antarctica. A part of her work questioned a standard assumption many models make about Greenland's climate history—the melting of the Greenland ice cap some 120,000 years ago when the climate was much warmer (up by 5°C). The sea levels did rise some five or six metres higher then, but not as a consequence of melting. Most likely for a wholly different reason. It was fascinating to hear her. It seemed good science to me.

Annabel smiled, stood up abruptly, and headed toward the refrigerator to bring me strawberries. The fruit basket in the fridge didn't look fresh, but I was unable to say no as she was eager that I taste those organic strawberries grown in California.

The tap in the bathroom had gone silent. Now it was free for me to use.

I had no intention of invading her privacy. The entrance to the bathroom was via the bedroom.

"Think I must be going."

"Sorry, today is a bit rushed."

She hovered around the kitchenette sink. Looking for a knife, perhaps, to cut strawberries. She could not see me. I had forgotten to ask if I could shadow a researcher in her ice core lab. I had been meaning to ask a favour really ever since my arrival at the conference. I needed her permission to shadow someone in the lab in order to perform a "literary experiment." But now was not the time to raise the delicate question. Based on the rapport we had developed, I knew the permission was almost a done deal. Perhaps call her in three or four days? She was a busy woman. My boots were on the mat near the door, I was wearing thick Scandinavian socks, and in those thick Scandinavian socks I rushed toward the bathroom as it was no longer possible to control myself.

On the way I encountered a bed and on the bed a half-undressed man. His neck long and thick. His chest hair gaping at me. I saw only one leg with a short little violin-shaped wound; otherwise it had almost no hair, as if he had shaved it all.

"The entrance." He pointed.

"What?"

"The bathroom entrance."

I locked the door without making much noise and made sure it was well locked. From inside I heard sounds of feet and voices and whispers. Annabel Sotto and Amitabh Ghosh.

I could hardly make out a word or two.

I looked at myself in the mirror coated with white toothpaste marks; my body was there and not there.

Turning on cold water I washed my hands. My face looked dry. The sink and the area under the sink nearly flooded as I washed my face. I seemed to have forgotten that I was in Canada with its dry washrooms. Back in India I used to wet my face exactly like this during long train journeys.

I looked at the mirror again. Saw Lucia. Demanding something, begging me, reminding me that her face deserved empathy just like all the other faces seen from up close.

When I left the bathroom, I didn't find Ghosh in the suite bedroom or the living area. I did not know whether to apologize to Annabel or to him. "Time to go." I dashed to the door and put on my muddy footwear.

He came out, fully dressed, and asked me to stay; he said he had something to tell me, something important.

"Tomorrow would be good," I said, emphasizing every word. I returned to my room.

Five or six minutes later there was a knock on my door. I dreaded that knock.

It was the room service. They had forgotten to replace the towels. Four or five unnecessary towels. And a fresh cake of soap. I requested they leave behind two bags of herbal tea.

"What kind, ma'am?"

"Doesn't matter."

Soon after, another knock.

Annabel and Amitabh.

Hurriedly they entered and shut the door behind them. He did not even wait to sit down.

"Lucia and I don't have a relationship the way it seems. You must be shocked. If I were you, I would be shocked as well. All I would like to say is that you have just met Lucia and you don't know many things about us. I would like to request you keep this to yourself. It is a long story and incredibly easy to explain. If you let her know, she will hurt and I will hurt and so will the children and so will Anna."

She was silent most of the time and kept clearing some dandruff-like particles from her blue T-shirt.

He lacked hesitation, the kind of hesitation I have seen in men, Canadian and Indian.

After they left, I skipped dinner and went to bed early. Sleep did not arrive right away. How was I supposed to proceed? How to tell my new friend Lucia what I had witnessed? Perhaps it was not a good idea to unsettle her before hearing his reasons.

One must never look at a face from so close, especially not the face of a stranger, even if it could not be helped, even if one has to suffer for a while, even if it is done on someone else's behalf, because everything that takes place in the kind of world we live in has consequences, and at times even the seemingly small consequences can become something really large.

■ ■ ■

Next morning I woke up early and walked along the lake and listened to the silence and noise of the landscape. Echoes of a waterfall. Ribbon-like clouds, twisted and involuntarily caught in the gaps between mountains and roofs of cottages, looked strangely beautiful. I returned to the conference for a buffet breakfast with a Bulgarian geology professor. The main event of the day was a brief moment when I sighted Annabel at a distance. She smiled. I walked up to her; we talked about the Burgess Shale hiking trail closure everyone was talking about. The park warden wanted to reduce contact between humans and wildlife for a week. Other than that I wrote a few impressions in my notebook. My head kept aching mildly. I did not feel like sitting through presentations or networking. Before driving back I took a tablet and coffee and wandered through the jungle of conference posters on display. Graduate student posters, some of them overtly ambitious, on known and unknown topics. How much Anthropocene? When did it begin? Technofossils. Cloud brightening. Detecting undetectable CO_2. Disappearing Tuvalu. Ocean fertilization. Habitat loss after the Great Acceleration. Planeticide. The End of Nature. Is James Hansen's Venus Syndrome speculation reasonable? Is the Anthropocene a retooling of Imperial Geology? Do we come from *Hallucigenia* or *Pikaia*? Contingency in Earth's history. Geo-bio-ethics. Nine geological commandments for *sapiens* in order to return to Holocene.

■ ■ ■

On the way back I received two phone calls, one from Lucia, but I ignored them both. Traffic moved at a slower pace for some unknown reason. Briefly I stopped at the same gas station. This time going against rigorous personal norms, I bought a bottle of Coke and two bags of Miss Vickie's salt-and-vinegar chips. The man at the cash was a middle-aged refugee from Tuvalu, an island nation near New Zealand just about to be drowned as a result of climate change.

Unimagining

15

Today, after discarding the unopened bottle of Coke, I skimmed through a marvellous book, *Earth Emotions: New Words for a New World*, by the philosopher Glenn Albrecht. While savouring the pages of this urgent book I found an incredible word:

"*Solastalgia*—the pain or distress caused by the loss or lack of solace and the sense of desolation connected to the present state of one's home and territory. It is the lived experience of the negative environmental change. It is the homesickness you have when you are still at home."

Today I thought of making a delicious mango salsa salad for myself. Something that looks beautiful with beautiful ingredients. Something easy on me. But. I remain painfully aware that it would be impossible to eat and smell such things again.

Today I wrote: I have no option but to resign myself absolutely to pure hunger and pure thirst.

Today there is a fly in my room. Wings akimbo. Now and then it gets agitated. The sounds it produces are exact imitations of electric sparks.

Today I laughed a lot when I misspelled the common word (in many North Indian languages) for *ghost*.

Today I am trying to forget Amitabh Ghosh and Annabel Sotto.

Today I made a resolve to avoid all things global and solar. I don't want to be burned by the sun of sciences.

■ ■ ■

The fondest memories of my childhood are myths, folk and fairy tales, Panchatantra fables, and Kathasaritsagara (Ocean of the Rivers of Stories). When it came to mathematics, I knew the names of a few ancient Indian mathematicians. Regarding the sciences, other than a few calendar images of bald and turbaned and curly-haired national scientists, most stories revolved around Darwin, Madam Curie, Einstein, and so on. The way the Indian scientist story was told was via the glories and recognition received in the Western world, not the way a typical so-called Western scientist's story is told—via obstacles faced by an individual, who almost gets burned on the stake by the church or dominant ideology before the crowning achievement.

■ ■ ■

Where I grew up this model of storytelling was popular, however, to remember the lives of Bhakti and Sufi saints. Kabir, Mira Bai, and Nanak, for instance, the ones who fearlessly questioned religious and caste orthodoxy. Moving to Canada made me encounter yet another type of story: the way the Western scholars narrated the Indian scientist, a narration that lacked empirical work and relied more on provincialism, ignorance, and absurd generalizations. I also figured that in the so-called West (euphemism for *white*) certain problematic aspects of a celebrated scientist got expunged from his life story, transforming him into a "saint" who could never have sinned. For instance, Charles Lyell could not have been the same man who was also hell-bent on naturalizing colonialism. One reads textbooks of geology, but one rarely reads the actual biography of geology, its omissions, its caste system and "sedimented non-events."

■ ■ ■

The struggle between humans and power is not simply the struggle between memory and forgetting (i.e., the remembrance of science past). The struggle is also the struggle between "imagining" and "unimagining."

Today I am trying to process the ruins, the traces, the bones of Dr. G: the big public story I never got to formulate properly.

I hear his faint voice as persistent as a housefly.

How one becomes what one is. I ask him. I ask myself.

He clings to the evolving stories of all his students—several batches—as if he were some mythical Bara-Deo, the one who created living breathing creatures out of his own sweat.

Even students like Gauri, who made a clean break, find it difficult to be completely rid of his presence.

Even I, the one who winnowed away, am his consequence.

He is like a haystack packed inside a needle. The needle pierces one no matter where one escapes.

I imagined G in a particular way, but now I keep trying to unimagine him. I imagined science in a certain way, but now I try to unimagine that so I am able to locate the process and diagram the mechanism.

Unimagining in no way means the end of stories. When we read we sometimes feel the temptation to skip the story to the end. Unimagining is skipping the story to the beginning. To a beginning.

How does one unimagine Dr. G et al. in an *uneven* world of science? I can begin with the givens. The world of the sciences is what it is, and it is not going to change the way a character changes in a novel. Two things are given: (1) How amazingly international and interconnected the sciences are—without borders and with territory as large as the cosmos—and yet how utterly small and provincial and nationalistic. (2) The scientific might of a nation is closely tied with its economic and military might.

Obviously, these givens in no way prevent me from unimagining. So why am I still facing a strange inner resistance?

In my heart I know the kind of writing I have set out to do will be neither honest nor truthful if I don't confront the source of the resistance. Perhaps all the embodied childhood nationalism alerts me that a certain type of reader would treat G as a single story about Indian science, and I find myself obliged to provide glorious examples from the country of my birth—a Raman, a Khorana, a Bose of Higgs-boson fame, etc. But I don't want to spend a lifetime fussing about the unevenness of science; I don't feel like playing this game as if I were some Disney character.

Why can't I be more like the novelists from privileged countries who get to ignore stuff like this? They imagined science in a particular way, and I read them a lot in my younger years. They fabricated the world of science for me, and I took the trails using their imaginary maps; me, a brown girl, would walk and run or take trains and fly through the so-called universal imagination. But there was a problem. Always the brown girl had to figure out when the word *man* in a novel meant "all humans" and when it meant "a white man"; when the word *woman* meant "all women" and when it meant "a white woman."

■ ■ ■

Back to task. In a novella all I can really do is focus on something concrete, less abstract, and I have chosen a housefly; my main focus is going to be the fly in my room, the one that is bugging me right now. Buzzing in my left ear. At the moment there are two houseflies in my room: G and his detractor.

G buys a fossil from a shop in Paris and claims he dug it up in the Himalayas. He steals one from a lab in Wales and reports that he located it in the Himalayas. He moves a fragile fish fossil from China and sketches high Himalayas, etc.

Voice of Dr. T, the whistleblower, who shook Dr. G's kingdom:
(Australian Broadcasting Corporation archives)

". . . I'd started on a major project with colleagues at the Siberian branch of the Academy of Science in Novosibirsk, SIBERIA, looking at biogeography for a 100 million year time slice back in the deep past but we had this spurious data from G.

"So I finally decided in the beginning of 1987 that something had to be put into print, preferably obscurely.

"I targeted a conference that was being held in CALGARY and prepared a presentation there, which included material from MOROCCO and material that was in one of the plates in a paper by G. And I was able to show these simultaneously on the screen, so the fossils in the two presentations looked exactly the same, and G was in the front row. One of my colleagues jumped up and said: Well, how do you explain having exactly the same fossils in two localities 600 kilometres apart? Now if that isn't a miracle I don't know what is.

"G stormed out of the room and he came back waving his fists and obviously wanted to punch me up but the crowd, there were about 250 there, just closed in and he couldn't get near me. He did this three times and then he demanded from the organisers a list of everyone that was at the meeting and he wanted a copy of my manuscript, but fortunately the director of the Senckenberg Museum in FRANKFURT said, Do you want me to publish it? And I said, Yes. . ."

What happened to you as the whistleblower? Were there any dire consequences or were you a hero for having done this?

"Oh, I don't know about a hero. There were no particularly dire consequences, just a few death threats. The people who were hurt most were in INDIA.

"His technician said at morning tea in G's department, G wasn't present, he said, 'I know where practically everything came from, I know where he hooked material out of books and so on'. He said, 'I've got a story to tell, I'm going to tell it', and the following night he was killed in a hit and run accident.

"G offered monies to anyone who would inflict grievous bodily harm on my honorary authors of the original monograph on this published by the Senckenberg Museum in FRANKFURT and a colleague at the Geological Survey in India took a bus three and a half hours to inform them, these two, to be very careful when and where they went. And about ten days later the mother of one of them was skittled in a hit and run accident, both legs, both arms broken, eight or ten ribs broken and she went into immediate senile decline after this traumatic experience."

Such a tale, one of the saddest in the sciences, could never compete with *The Wizard of Oz*. But it was not entirely forgotten. For one brief day in the early twenty-first century Dr. G made big news all over again.

Twenty-six years after the conference in Calgary, the Palaeontological Society of India published a tiny booklet that made a half-hearted attempt to tell the story.

Ignoring the recommendations of a High Court judge (who chaired the four-year-long inquiry), Panjab University gave permission to G to retain his professorship, and hang onto the PhD and Doctor of Science degrees, both based on questionable work.

The institute did request him to stop doing palaeontology.

So *our man* reinvented himself in a reconstituting world as a professor of ground water geology (and global warming) instead. In the same department. Soon after, as I found out from other sources, he started churning out *books* on climate change.

What a waste, I thought. The kind of possibilities that existed for a project like *Himalayan Fossil Fraud* were immense. It never occurred to the Palaeontological Society to include personal testimonies of hundreds of scientists involved—directly or indirectly—with Dr. G.

The tiny booklet was too little, too late, and filled with its own silences and inaccuracies even as it aspired to clear up things.

But at least it is there. For those who go by self-correction and geoethics to continue the work.

By the time I tried to sketch Dr. G's portrait (ironically in a work of fiction) he had already retired. I tried to locate him. He lives in the outskirts of Chandigarh now where five irrigation canals meet—Panchkula—and not in that bungalow on campus.

Why don't I let him be in the outskirts?

Websites informed me that our man's "books" on global warming are available in libraries all over the globe, including in Berlin and Istanbul. Shoddy, opportunistic collections of cut-and-paste magazine articles, not based on actual research. Ironically, in one volume he expressed concern over an American president's deception "to *kill* the Kyoto protocol."

Even his old con, books on geology and palaeontology and stratigraphy, and most of his papers—published nationally and internationally—continue to circulate.

Cited by thousands of authors.

Quoted by hundreds.

Geologists say "data contamination" of this kind lasts for decades, at times for a couple of centuries. The books and papers carry no warning. We have no idea if G ever read the great writer Borges, who loved to manufacture evidence and exulted in creation of fabulous histories. In one Borgesian world G has still not been exposed. In another he will be exposed exactly four hundred years from now.

■ ■ ■

From my old handwritten journal:

> Obstacles toward unimagining the great man: I worry an entire generation at Panjab University might have learned climate change from Dr. G.
>
> The real tragedy: how difficult it has become for researchers in India to have their work accepted in prestigious international journals. Rafat Azmi, the palaeontologist who discovered a 1.6-billion-year-old alga, was suspected of fraud by his peer reviewers; it took years to establish innocence and accomplishment.

■ ■ ■

My colleagues at the Chandigarh-based newspaper the *Tribune* made attempts on my behalf; one encountered G at a funeral and requested an interview. Dr. G declined. Not unexpected. So I imagined and unimagined our meeting. That is all one can do in such situations. Hold conversations. Not without empathy, karuna, and compassion.

One night, unable to sleep, I thought of composing a novella from the point of view of his dead mother. She, clad in a white sari, was a sagely character, but I failed to capture her voice properly.

G walks through the modern streets and sectors of Chandigarh. It is 45°C. But it feels like 52°C because the hot and dry wind—the loo—is blowing. I watch him drink sugar-cane juice from a roadside vendor by the rose garden. His hand is sticky. We engage in small talk under the shade of a struggling tree.

"What made you do all this?"

"Your entire case against me," he says, "is based on flawed ideas about 'self-correction' in science."

G quotes an expert in his defence: "Opinions (in science) converge not because bad data is corrected but because it is swamped."

"Your mother has a few questions for you," I say.

"But she is dead," he corrects me.

"The dead ask some of the finest questions," I remind him in his mother's voice. "Son of mine, were you ever worried that you might get exposed? What was it like to continue with your colleagues and students after you were caught? How did you prepare your face to face them nearly every day? How do you look your wife and children in the eye? Son, do you ever see the face of the murdered lab assistant?"

■ ■ ■

Then there were questions not for him but for those around him.

How come no Indian scientist managed to blow the whistle for such a long period of time? Prestigious journals? International co-authors? How many Gs exist in any given country at any given time?

I discussed the case with two friends, both sociologists, one in India and one in Canada. When I talk to them, I always feel sociologists have answers to everything. Both pointed out the culture of "obedience." Both emphasized that G's thesis supervisor—trained at a university in the United Kingdom—had a pet geological theory that could only be validated if the graduate student in India found a graptolite fossil in the Kashmir Himalayas.

■ ■ ■

How did he feel as a grad student after the first peripatetic fossil? What made him repeat the wicked technique in all its variations over and over? How does one become what one is?

"Many," he says, "never get exposed. But I didn't know this when I started. Only my professor *knew* things; I just had to *confirm* what he knew. I was young. My job was to *please* him. If I saw something in a rock that he didn't *see*, then that thing didn't exist. My job was to see what he *saw*."

"You figured out how to play the game?" I say. "You figured out how to replace the king. You managed to suppress other young rivals. One day you established your own kingdom?"

"What if," he says, "someone else found a real fossil in the same area where I found an unreal fossil? Perhaps I was confident that at least one person would find a real fossil after me. No one would have called me a fake after the discovery of *that* real fossil. You would have given me a Vetlesen Prize instead, the Nobel for geology."

"Evidential traces of a gambler in you?" I say.

"My motives were not entirely financial," he says. "I wanted to be famous. I wanted my country to be extraordinarily famous."

■ ■ ■

On close examination the scientific papers suggest the Prince of Himalayan Geology lacked a basic knowledge of chemistry and physics. "Not an accomplished forger." A fish fossil (say) found in Marrakesh is always supposed to be different from one found in the Himalayas, for it is in a different state of preservation.

Chandan S. Mani, a young historian who is in the process of revising a two-volume science encyclopaedia, informed me that Dr. G had aversion toward people he considered lower castes. He, like several other respectable and enlightened names in the country, felt "lower castes" and "peasants" contaminated knowledge and the sciences. "Reserved-category people," he called them. "Sweepers" and "brainless truck drivers," he called them. Only fit to become lab technicians.

So famous he became that he was allowed to make major changes in textbooks of palaeontology that are essential reading for all geology students in India. Every year the government consulted Professor G to set the paper for the civil services exam.

"Who discovered the oldest fish from India?"

The key question was not *who discovered* the oldest fish. The fish must have made Borgesian demands on geologists to tell the story of our planet and the story of life a little differently.

With time he acquired courage and higher levels of ambition, authoring multiple papers with the same fake object (and its photographs), in essence suggesting that he found a unique specimen at more than one site, sites far apart.

He *discovered* stunning things in areas considered unfossiliferous. But he must have thought through carefully. Finding a fossil in an unfossiliferous zone gives it a rare aura and puzzles theorists for decades.

■ ■ ■

The reason I did not include G's tale in my article on "self-criticism of science" was part personal, part creative, a crisis. I could not find an appropriate model for his story, neither in India nor in Canada, nor in my thick personal file labelled "Prominent cases of scientific irregularities." Some 2,022 cases. The list is incredibly diverse and keeps widening like oil sands tailings ponds up north. The names in the list rhyme as if they were an essential part of an epic poem————————Marc Hauser, Yoshitaka Fujii, Jon Sudbo, Alfred Fusco, Dong-Pyou Han, Gideon Koren, Masoumeh Ebtekar, Eric Smart, Luk Van Parijs, Joachim Boldt, Sophina (Sophie) Jamal, John Darsee, Jan Hendrik Schön, Milena Penkowa, Erin Potts-Kant, Santosh Katiyar, Dipak Das, William Gass . . .

I read a sad case from Spain. Five co-authors used the reputation of a recently dead author, Dr. Margarita Lázaro, to publish a big paper. I became aware, rather well aware, of the North American affairs as well. The oil and gas exploitation engineer John Macdonald's tale and Felderhof, the polite Canadian geologist who "salted" a mysterious mining site with gold during the 1990s and milked over six billion dollars.

At the suggestion of a journalist colleague I studied the "fodder scam" story, which involved transfer of funds into a politico's pockets, funds reserved for procuring fodder for cows that did not exist or existed only on paper.

Obviously, I saw some parallels, but G's tale belongs to a very different class of narratives. About time to switch, I thought. And I switched to fiction, to literary truths and reflections, the novel in all its variations, including the novel-as-it-transforms-itself facing the Anthropocene, the novel as it awakens itself, and this continues to provide me, rather allow me—despite an irreversible change in my condition—remarkable tools to imagine and unimagine. It also provides me a home. Without the novel I am homeless.

■ ■ ■

Years before the conference in Calgary, the whistle-blower from Oz, Dr. T, visited Gauri's and my university in Chandigarh "to touch" the graptolite fossil with his own hands. Dr. G's UK-trained thesis supervisor had long retired by then. G was in his office playing dominoes with a large collection of keys. For obvious reasons he declined Dr. T's request. As a compensation he regaled the visitor with a story. "That day because of vehicular problems and inclement weather I arrived rather late in Kashmir. The light was part pointillist, part crepuscular. A pony was waiting for me by the bus stop. The ground was slippery, but I did not heed the warning. The trail cut through a dark forest full of bears. Suddenly the pony shook violently. I fell down the ravine into a glacial stream of water. Fortunately, some eight or nine hundred metres later I was able to hold on to a craggy rock, my last hope to survive. And there they were, swarms of strange-looking flies, and there they were, the graptolite fossils, right under my nose. Beckoning, saying to me with little ghostly voices, 'Cheer up, young man, here is your chance to serve geology.'"

■ ■ ■

The flies in my room continue to be fruitful. They caress the transparent window glass, saying something to it with their eloquent halteres. But soon they run out of patience and choose the collision course. Do they want something from me more than the usual in-house observations? *Musca domestica.* How fast they multiply and acquire flesh; I am amazed. Amazed not just by the greatest show on Earth, but also by people who study it. There is a Dr. G, a Dr. T, and then there is a mildly ambitious Dr. B.

Dr. B is the chief editor of a prestigious journal. Dr. B is also the director of a museum of natural history. He is a gold card–carrying member with several airlines and flies around globally. While he facilitates the publication of Dr. T's articles like "The Case of the Peripatetic Fossils," it may never occur to him that the word *peripatetic*, for a reader like me, has yet another meaning.

"Palaeontology is trying," says Chandan S. Mani, the historian of science. "But the discipline has not been able to decolonize. . . . The fossils that rich countries move from poor countries to their educational institutions and museums don't count as problematic. It rarely occurs to a natural history museum in London or Washington or Berlin, that a part of their collection came from other countries.

"In the Anthropocene we need to develop imaginative responses. We need to form a planetary agency, different from the UN, in order to facilitate ethical research. . . . Delivering geoethical commandments to world citizenry is useless if scientists themselves don't do science ethically.

"In the Anthropocene it becomes unacceptable to look the other way when toxic scientific waste and equipment gets shipped to poor countries for burial or scavenging."

I nod in agreement. Today I am thinking about the future. Would there ever be a time when I get to say there are no more of them? I am done with houseflies, I would like to say.

Today I read about Herton Escobar, a Brazilian science journalist colleague of mine, who had interviewed yet another type of fly: a palaeobiologist at a prestigious university in the UK. Dr. D is a rising research star. Dr. D dismissed questions about his team's lack of collaboration with Brazilian researchers on a specimen found there. "I mean, do you want me to also have a Black person on the team for ethnicity reasons, and a cripple and a woman, and maybe a homosexual too just for a bit of all-round balance?"

Today my eyes are filled with a slim film of moisture. Hidden in the film there are hints of gladness. Glad I don't have to interact with certain faces of palaeontology and evolutionary biology—faces only slightly different from Georges-Louis Leclerc (Comte de Buffon, 1707–1788), Louis Agassiz (1807–1873), and Ernst Haeckel (1834–1919)—the ones who saw a section of *sapiens* as "pure and superior" and others as "impure and degenerated." Today I am trying to forget the so-called gentlemanly face of Sir Roderick Murchison (1792–1871)—an active participant in imperial expansion and violence because it was "good for geology." There is a mountain peak named after him in the Canadian Rockies.

What I am trying to say and finding it difficult to say is that scientific racism doesn't stop within the disciplinary boundaries. Racist ideas developed by scientists benefit a certain section of *sapiens*; they penetrate, "contaminate" entire ecosystems, even the fields of memory, imagination, speculation, and literature. H.G. Wells's *The Time Machine* was heavily influenced by the so-called degeneration theory, as I learned recently.

Even in our day and age, so-called artificial intelligence finds itself contaminated (to use Dr. T's pet word). Machines are being wilfully taught racist and sexist algorithms. Facebook users viewing video clips of Black men were asked by an autogenerated prompt if they would like to "keep seeing videos about primates."

Old technologies: The camera was never neutral. Optimized for white skin colour, photography has been heavily complicit. New technologies: The "impartiality" of algorithms is false.

While I support Dr. T's whistle-blowing, I have problems with his use of words like *purity* and *contamination*. *Contamination*—many a time—makes me think of caste system and degeneration theory.

Let me be clear. None of them—Dr. T, Dr. B, Dr. D—subscribes to the nineteenth-century variety of scientific racism. Yet none of them seems to be tormented by systemic problems within the sciences.

Dr. G gets singled out. Dr. B and other enablers remain invisible. The problems in the discipline will not vanish by simply removing an occasional contaminant. Today my tongue is free. My lips unbuttoned. Today I no longer struggle to whisper in the ears of the dying, and the unborn. Good science remains entangled with multiple things one would like to condemn. For a start it would be helpful to simply acknowledge plain facts, and not become defensive with erroneous statements like "Science is autonomous and pure and it has no culture or ideology."

Today I am glad to condemn Dr. G, but I would be equally glad to see entire communities condemn the vast web of systemic problems in the sciences. Who knows, some day people might step out on the streets and demolish certain statues.

16

For us geologists every bit of space keeps becoming time. A little piece of rock is a little piece of rock, but also a little piece of time. When we glue two or three rocks together, we are also (knowingly or unknowingly) gluing time with time, and time within time.

■ ■ ■

Two students in our class quit toward the end of semester. One started dressing in saffron clothes and joined a religious cult, and the other joined his father's business. Most of us graduated, scattered to different cities and continents. By this time Gauri and Vikram Jit or Ruby had largely faded from everyday conversations.

Then the sightings began. Always from a distance. Always ambiguous.

Someone saw Vikram Jit in Chandigarh. Someone saw or almost saw him in the US, in Canada.

Most grad students not *lucky* enough to get direct admission into a US university moved from Chandigarh to the US via Canada. But Vikram Jit (or his ghost), according to one highly questionable account, had shifted from India to the US to Canada. No one knew any details of what he did in Canada, where he was based, whether he was still in the sciences. "I saw him in London in Canada or boarding the Queen Street streetcar in Toronto, but before I could make contact he had disappeared."

Two ex-classmates of mine, now based in the US, tried to locate more; they found nothing. The image I was given was that of an inmate in the film *One Flew Over the Cuckoo's Nest*, the one inmate who managed to escape to Canada. With time they stopped following Vikram Jit's trail because there was no trail. He was dead.

■ ■ ■

How I established that Lucia's husband, Amitabh Ghosh, and Ruby (or Vikram Jit) were one and the same person is rather complicated and unsettling and required an entirely different type of excavation, drilling, and stratigraphy. Here, I relate the medium-long version. Of course, seeing him half-dressed or half-naked in Annabel Sotto's room made me less and less unsure. His body was his face, more than his actual face.

Four things happened during (and after) the conference that provided traces of evidence.

First. During his talk he had used a slim black marker to diagram a thought experiment on the whiteboard. His handwriting had a peculiar smallness and tightness that was vaguely familiar.

Second. During the Q and A right after his talk on geoengineering, a middle-aged man in an Armani jacket made an off-the-cuff comment: ". . . and just like South Asians happen to be natural-born Silicon Valley computer wizards, now one will have to add Anthropocene science and engineering to the ever-growing list." Those patronizing words generated a wave of uneasy laughter. I don't think anyone took offence. Ironically, the response of those visibly South Asian seemed to be the exact opposite, the response of pride.

It was then that a curious grad student from London, Ontario, asked the presenter about the institute where Amitabh Ghosh got his undergrad degree. His response was a bit baffling, at least to my ears. "Institutions do not matter," he said, tactfully steering the discussion to individuals, etc. This was followed by two or three lines on the self-taught genius mathematician Ramanujan, plus a recommendation to go watch the film about him.

Third. The little violin-shaped wound on his leg. When I was young, I didn't know how to describe someone naked, especially a man. Gauri was no better. This is how she had described his genital area to me a few days after they slept together. That evening in Annabel's hotel room I saw two violin-shaped wounds. The first one was Gauri's euphemism of a metaphor. The second one, a literal wound, a scar. Two classmates of mine had bandaged Ruby when he fell on the tracks not long after

Gauri's passing. During our return train journey they had described the wound as deep, something shaped like a musical instrument. Can you be more specific? A short little violin.

Fourth. Before I spell it out—the definitive proof—I must set it out.

■ ■ ■

Fourth. Around the time of the conference, without a sufficient warning, my father visited me in Calgary. I kept the heat cranked up during his visit and found myself going through the learning curve of how to share private space. We both knew by now the unspoken reason for his sudden arrivals, his gentle attempts to persuade me to get married.

The magazine deadlines (as usual) were keeping me busy. I called a colleague to check if he could give my father a tour of the city. My colleague was on a deadline as well.

Lucia had phoned me then to discuss something about the workshop, and reluctantly I asked if she would be able to take my old man out one day.

She agreed.

I did not want Father to get involved in her complicated life. But I thought this would send a clear message to Amitabh Ghosh that I had decided to guard the information I was privy to, that I was willing to wait for him to contact me and reveal more about his relationship with Lucia.

The two of them collected Father one morning and drove him to the art museum, and then to a dim-sum place in Chinatown.

I spent the whole day processing a story about an illegal ocean fertilizing experiment carried out by a Canadian scientist in British Columbia. Russ George, the rogue engineer, the Pacific Ocean Hacker. While gathering facts I stumbled across other facts, even more inconvenient. The two superpowers (US and USSR) wondered about new ways to kill during the Cold War years—how does one weaponize weather? Is it possible to bring about droughts and floods in the land of one's foe by manipulating weather?

The father of the hydrogen bomb, Edward Teller, proposed weather manipulation as a new kind of warfare. A Soviet scientist proposed injecting thirty-six million tonnes of aerosols into the stratosphere.

One thing led to another. At NASA some scientists engaged with interplanetary studies (especially Mars and Venus) turned their attention to Earth. What they found about our planet's climate systems was worrisome.

This is how Earth systems science came into being. Loops, cycles, interactions, links, feedbacks positive and negative, non-linearity, tipping point. This is a watershed moment in the discipline of geology.

I knew I had to ask Lucia's husband pointed questions about such complex, ironic, and brutal histories.

Personally, I found it a bit confusing: geoengineering led to climate science led to geoengineering.

Hurriedly I jotted down my initial list of questions for the husband's interview.

She phoned me right after they dropped my father back. "Thank you." She thanked me profusely *for such a good time. Your old man regaled the children with stories. Later at the museum gift shop we found him flirting with a sixty-year-old woman! Most hearts grow young with age,* she said.

I looked at my father. He had popped back into the apartment happy.

He never remarried. I don't know the exact reason. I never asked.

Our relationship is not entirely without wrinkles. When I was young the general rule was to ignore stuff that caused arguments, but at some point, I stopped avoiding it.

He listens to me and gives the impression that he is going to change, he tells me a good story, and we forget the episode. Compared to my mother he has always been a superior teller of oral tales. Before she died, Mother revealed a secret. Something not shared with anyone in the family.

She didn't know much science. Ma was as unscientific as love between parents and children. University was still a year away. I would do my homework quietly so as not to disturb my sickly mother. One night after giving her medicines, I sat by the edge of her bed. The room had a sharp odour. She said she wanted to share something important.

"Perhaps you can do so tomorrow."

"No, no, you daughter of mine. Just sit down. I must tell you now, for tomorrow would be too late.

"The story involves two brothers.

"I was supposed to marry your uncle.

"The two families had fixed our wedding, but I was in love with your uncle's younger brother, the railway man. As the wedding date approached my saheli (*girlfriend*) teased, 'At least you will be living close to your beloved.' My sadness grew. I felt trapped inside a bad movie. I imagined the premature death of the prospective bridegroom. The death of your uncle.

"There was yet another possibility to eliminate suffering: my own death. For nine or ten nights, every midnight I would slip out of the house and stand by the village well. Unable to kill myself, I fell sick. There was debilitating weakness, high fever, 104, and hallucinations, and a plan."

Ma squeezed my arm. Not sure if she was consoling me or herself. Every cell in my body felt like crying. She was dying. There was a strange urgency in her voice.

"When I shared 'the plan' with my saheli," Ma continued, "she warned that I would eventually get caught and this would cause lifelong frictions. Dayan, they would call me."

"Dayan?"

"Witch."

"The plan?" I asked my mother.

"Of course, I will tell you. But first, tell, did you ever detect any friction between your uncle's family and ours?"

"Ours is a happy family."

Ma's smile brightened and enlarged the room.

"We, my saheli and I, enlisted an eighty-year-old woman as an ally. She lived on the third floor of a haveli in the village, a house she rarely left. Rumours started spreading from the haveli that the woman had read my fortune and found it to be a piece of shit. That I would not be able to bear children. Not with any man."

Ma laughed and coughed. I gave her water. She could not drink more than a sip.

"Your uncle's family lost interest. But his younger brother—your papa—defied his family's wishes."

"So," I asked Ma, "Father knew all along that you had enlisted the eighty-year-old?"

"As a matter of fact, no. I was going to tell him. Tempted at the same time to test how much he loved me."

She paused for a while.

"But you told him later?"

"One delay led to another. Soon you were born."

"So, when did you?"

"This I have held on to all these years."

Not long after, my mother passed away. Whenever I was upset, Father consoled me: "She will come back within a few years. Mother is getting treatment in a special hospital in a city far away in some foreign land."

What I want to say and am having trouble saying is that there are lies we tell knowingly and lies we tell unknowingly. What I want to say is that there are lies that come to us from older generations. Some get transmitted knowingly and others unknowingly. What I want to say is that there are lies that save lives, and lies that harm others (and us). Lies that bring people together.

What I want to say is that we lie not just with our words, but also with our silences.

Like my mother, I have been unable to share the secret.

I took my father to a three-star Vietnamese restaurant with the intention of telling him everything over there.

I knew he was going to ask me about marriage as always, but not right away. He had tried almost every way to initiate the conversation. This time he began by asking something I was not prepared for.

"Have I been a good father?"

Marriage for him means children, and this shut me off for a while. My mother would not have understood my decision either. But we two could have tried to have a proper conversation about marriage at least over the phone.

When I started paying attention to my father's words again, he was talking about something poles apart. Turner and his paintings. At the art museum he had looked at *Chichester Canal* (1829), *The Slave Ship* (1840), *Sunset, Fighting Bucks* (1829), and a "storm painting" by the British painter.

The Year Without a Summer, 1816, I almost said to him. Turner's stunning sunsets, among other things, convey remarkable info to scientists and detectives about planetary cooling caused by past volcanic eruptions, I almost said.

"A painting of a storm based on a real storm," Father said. "The painter made his ship captain tie him to the mast with a tight rope so that he could observe minutely, without taking shelter or fleeing to safety. What Turner wanted to see was the eye of a real storm."

Standing before the paintings Lucia must have pointed out a few details my father had missed: the artist's intention or his friendships with scientists or the strange colours of sunsets or the social conditions. Although he doesn't dwell much in the past, Father must have listened to her patiently, nodding his head now and then when she used words like "Victorian England," because all of a sudden, my father was talking Victorian and coal.

"Both your friends are very knowledgeable. And well settled. They made a wise decision to get married and have children. The children are very smart. They have a much better Canadian accent. I had a good conversation with Dr. Ghosh as well. He knows a lot about coal."

"Coal?"

Because this was the third time the waiter made it to our table, both of us felt it would be wise to order. Father did not want glass noodles as usual (they stick to his moustache). He insisted that I order for both of us. The waiter wrote with a short little pencil—spicy lemon-grass chicken, seafood platter, papaya salad, sticky rice.

"Dr. Ghosh studied coal in India."

"Institute?"

"What do you mean?"

"University?"

My father failed to recall.

How in the world the wonderful waiter managed to serve us near instantaneously remains a mystery, but it seemed to me in the packed restaurant that my father's failure to recall was no mystery. Ghosh had employed the same tactic, but he had allowed something important to slip out. He told my father a story about his father.

"Dr. Ghosh's father was a senior manager at a big coal mine in Bengal," said my father. "You know *lignite*? Poorest rank of coal. It was that kind of a mine. Poor parents would come to the manager sa'ab nearly every day requesting, literally begging him to hire their unemployed sons to work at the dangerous mine. Dr. Ghosh's father had a thin skin when confronted by human suffering. A year later when a tragic explosion killed all the miners, he was devastated; he kept seeing their faces, young dusty faces, for he was the one who had hired them all. All of them had gone underground that day because he had hired them. He thought about the agonizing choices he had had to make just a few weeks ago—whom to hire and whom not to hire. Only one miner, a seventeen-year-old, survived. This boy fled from the hospital and moved to Bombay, where around a month later he died in a fireworks factory accident near Juhu Beach."

The only problem with this narrative was that it was not Lucia's husband's father's story.

Gauri had an anthropologist friend at the university in Chandigarh. Someone I did not get along with. Ghosh's story was the anthropologist's father's story. Gauri had told me all the major and minor details several times. The anthropology department was next door to the geology department. The anthropologist was writing a paper on fossil fuels in colonial India and he would ask Gauri and me a few basic questions. His teeth were always yellow and he was always smoking a bidi and always highly critical of British geologists who wholeheartedly supported the imperial project. "Cheerleaders of genocides, ecocides, and slow violence . . . These white scientists used the authority of science, especially the principles of superposition and biostratigraphy, to naturalize colonial expansion and extermination of Indigenous populations . . . The Indigenous were seen as 'primitive' older layers of rock, and the remarkable concepts the natives had developed were considered 'equally primitive,' not even worthy of discussion or argument . . . Scientists like Ernst Haeckel endorsed the so-called degeneration theory of racial origins and eugenics . . . They looked at the most authentic fossils and developed these ideas. So what guarantee do we have that contemporary scientists who look at the same fossils won't come up with equally crazy and harmful ideas?"

Anyways he was the one who had told us that not a whole lot of people in India burned coal before colonialism. Some even made necklaces and other ornaments out of coal.

After telling me what he believed to be Lucia's husband's father's story, my father wiped his lips with a napkin. "Did you know some of our Indian people made jewellery out of coal before the arrival of British?"

17

When past was present, it had a future, but it was not the same as this one—our present. Scientists, philosophers, and artists keep rephrasing this thought in myriads of ways. During my darkest moments I end up finding some consolation in this thought; it reminds me that nothing is predetermined.

I was still at the airport saying goodbye to my father when an email arrived from Vikram Jit that read, "Call as soon as possible."

A chill went down my spine. I saw a guard frisk my elderly father even after he had done the security screening. My father "randomly chosen." Things came out of his scuffed navy bag and were put back, with the same racially profiled violence, before his body was allowed to slowly disappear toward the apprehensive planes.

It was not *if*, but *when* I was going to see Vikram Jit.

Feeling unsafe, I delayed going back home. The airport shuttle had a small waiting area within the terminal building. I sat down. Performed a breathing exercise to deal with anxiety. Right after, I checked if all the features of my phone were functioning. The Wi-Fi connection was strong. For once I didn't mind all the surveillance cameras around me.

I was getting ready, almost ready.

I repeated the breathing exercise.

I am not opposed to all forms of artificial intelligence. What I oppose are the facial-recognition algorithms which come with serious racial and gender biases. The white male algorithms make serious errors. Errors different from the ones we ordinary humans make about face recognition in our everyday.

While researching my article on tech companies, I had encountered more material than I could process. In my published article I skipped the material on *dissociation*. Dissociative amnesia. The editor was not keen on raising the word limit, so I skipped a woman, an abused woman's story. It was certainly not a familiar story about textures and ambiguities of memory. The room where she was abused had a TV. She thought the newscaster's face on the screen was the face of the perpetrator. The "human error" shielded her from the stab of place-time she didn't want to go near; it helped her survive the event and the aftermath. Perhaps.

My situation was different. I didn't know where my dissociation was coming from.

Gauri's face, the face that used to form within me, started changing when she passed away.

What is strange is that Ruby or Vikram Jit's face also started changing right after. I could not look at him properly. When I tried staring, I felt his face was not his face.

Explanations come later. Sometimes far too late.

If there was dissociation, my dissociation, I was unaware of it. When I became partially aware, I didn't want to make an error about his face.

I wanted to be doubly certain.

I was almost ready.

I repeated the breathing exercise and started surfing. Aimless surfing through the web always calms me down.

I typed three random words (flamingos, India, eggs) on Google.

The article began with the unbearable lightness-beauty-sadness of migratory flamingos in the largely desolate Rann of Kutch. A large number of flamingos had abandoned their eggs in that part of India. The saltwater lagoons had dried up earlier than expected, and the birds disappeared, abandoning tens of thousands of eggs. The article mentioned the flying flamingos looked as if they were on fire.

I touched fire on the screen with the tip of my finger.

The article was linked to time (and its measurement). This surprised me. I continued reading.

"Our relationship with time could have been simpler, but it is not, and that is a good thing. How precise our ticking clocks have become, a mere second is as precise as 10 to the power of minus 19. . . . If in the olden days, time was a river, metaphorically speaking; now time is also a river, literally speaking."

These clocks, the article said, allow us to see the hidden rivers of water.

How was this connected to flamingos on fire?

I was almost ready, and continued reading.

Time, we know from Einstein, slows down with an increase in gravitational pull. This means any change in gravity will be detected by our clocks. Since the gravitational pull depends on mass, our clocks also detect the amount of mass that shifts in a particular location. We know now with the help of two extremely precise clocks (and satellites) that the groundwater level in North India is receding at the rate of twenty-five centimetres per year. We know now when the taps in Delhi will run dry. Tens of millions do not even have taps. We know now why the farmers are unhappy and out in the streets of the capital protesting.

My cellphone was ringing.

I ignored it a few times.

Three text messages followed.

I read the messages twice and opened my backpack and took out Gauri's tiny hand mirror and observed a face, my face, and adjusted my curly hair. I tilted the mirror a bit: a mother and a little girl and their luggage, on wheels. The little girl was moving her thumb and finger on the surface of the suitcase as if trying to zoom in.

The phone rang again.

The caller, at once familiar and unfamiliar to my ears, sounded charmingly agitated. He hung up, called again. We spoke.

I didn't want to go, but in the end, I decided to go ahead that very day. I wanted to see Amitabh Ghosh out in the open; we picked a downtown café. "See you in ninety minutes."

I took the shuttle from the airport. Got off in my neighbourhood, my usual stop. Instead of returning straight to my apartment (to prepare my face to meet a face) I walked along the Bow River. The river originates at the shrinking Bow Glacier in the Canadian Rockies. I sat down by the waters on a wound of a stone. Something about that space was very tender and enveloped me with latent indeterminate melancholy, a strange and familiar vibration.

I was ready.

I skipped my apartment.

I walked toward the Sunnyside station to take the train to downtown. It was going to take me ten minutes to the station.

The quality of light was unusually fragile, veils within veils and a hint of smoke. A pearl necklace of a woman in her thirties rushed out of an oldish building, got into a cactus-green SUV, and disappeared so fast I thought I was watching a movie. The big prairie sky had looked uncanny in one of her side mirrors. Streams of thoughts raced within me, creating a tremendous need to slow down my mind. I thought about the one thing I had really learned from Vikram Jit or Ruby. I don't know if it's good or bad, but it has been useful at times. One day he and Gauri and I were walking toward the library to study. I had forgotten to bring my library card and turned back. No need to turn back, he had said.

"Simply enter the library as if you own the bloody place."

The few days Vikram Jit was still alive after Gauri's death, what stands out in my mind is what we didn't do. I felt the need to hear more stories about her. Felt the need to hug him. I didn't. Once or twice the opportunity presented itself, but the prospective hug felt like a device to wound myself further rather than heal. One day he was working in a lab, listening to Springsteen on his miniature tape player, when the drill in his hand got mixed up with his lab coat and two or three big buttons fell on the floor. I heard his lab partner volunteering to repair the damaged coat. Instead of thanking her he banged his fist on the table. Two lines of brown glass bottles with organics shook heavily.

When I made it to the open-air Sunnyside station to hop on the train to downtown, I found something irregular—Vikram Jit or Amitabh Ghosh was already on the platform. It seemed he knew all my movements; he knew where I lived.

He placated my fears as soon as we shook hands. "We often park our car here, in the sprawling grocery store parking lot, then go to downtown."

His shoes had Kevlar laces. I didn't allow my gaze to linger on the shoes. At this point it was necessary to say what I had been rehearsing.

"My father returned happy. He enjoyed spending time with you and Lucia. You two are a *delight*, he said."

No need to give him the impression that I was

processing Vikram Jit's suicide; I badly wanted him to believe that the only thing eating my mind at that moment was his relationship with Lucia. That is how we had left our last conversation. I wanted him to take over and bare his soul. I was ready to hear.

I had only one precarious weapon: my smartphone secretly recording our conversation.

"Did your father talk a lot about the trip?"

"Wait a minute," I said, trying to locate something in my jacket pocket.

"Of course he told me a few things," I said. "He said he was still savouring the dim sum and the soup. But the thing he repeated over and over was how amazing your marriage was."

"Lucia and I are perfectly all right when we are with others. And especially when we are with our children."

There were schoolchildren on the platform, waiting. A homeless man was removing something from the bins.

Amitabh Ghosh sat down.

"Shall we talk a bit here?"

"Sure," I said and sat next to him.

Trains kept coming and going intermittently and we remained there "catching up," as they say.

■ ■ ■

Briefly I told him how impressed my father was by the children. "Father said while driving to the restaurant you and your eldest engaged in a proper scientific chat. He listened carefully but could not comprehend words like *chinook*. Your daughter not only explained the snow-eating chinook winds to my father but also the process of *sublimation*. Now he can't stop sending his WhatsApp group links on sublimation. He likes your family more than me!"

Vikram Jit absorbed every single word I delivered. All he wanted to talk about was my father.

By this time there was no fear in me. It had sublimated. I experienced sudden flashes of memories. Memories of the same Sunnyside station when it was covered with calf-deep snow. The winter solstice was fast approaching (-49°C with the wind chill). The overheated café nearby, where I had found lots of random info about the city.

From my slim green backpack I took out a copy of the diasporic magazine. He gazed at the partially visible cover trying to make sense.

"There is a nice photo of you and your wife in here! Low res black and white. But you look great together!"

He chose not to respond. At that moment his face looked as if it belonged to a taciturn man.

"Hope you are feeling all right?" I almost put a hand on his shoulder.

"On the contrary," he said. "Never felt like this before . . ."

"You can tell me all."

"I have never felt like this before, although I know this is not true."

I was thirsty, no water in the backpack.

"I am all ears."

"Your father is a remarkable man."

"Listen, Amitabh, I don't have much time today. Let's start."

"He doesn't withhold anything."

"Shall I start with a question or a comment?"

"What do you mean?"

"Stuff about your work. Excellent presentation on global cooling, by the way. *Impressive* is a small word. Something grand. Ambitious. Just the scale of it. It brings God and the transcendent back into the game. This is not a mere geologist making sense of some obscure fossils or moving them around. This is complete planetary redesign."

He had come to see me in casual clothes. His face moist with the right kind of moisturizers. Lips unchapped. Incipient bird-feet patterns beneath his eyes. Cologne, weaponized.

Lucia's name had already come up several times. I didn't know if she knew about this strange coffee meeting with her husband. I sent her a vague text. Twice, because it failed the first time. She called right after. She asked me where I was and what I was doing. I said I was interviewing someone and hung up.

To this day I have not been able to figure out why I did not say "interviewing someone you know," the correct follow-up to my text message.

"May I record? Some of it. Not all."

"I have not come for the interview. You know this."

"Please," I said. "Before we talk about the affair, could I pick your brain about the Cold War histories of dimming the sun?"

"I am not here for histories of dimming."

A train passed by. He moved closer. I thought he was going to hug me or kiss me or hurt me.

"Of course, Lucia," I said, "knows nothing."

"So far."

"So far."

"I know," he said. "One reason I wanted to see you is because we must clarify a few things. In the spirit of clarification I have a few questions. Tell me, how come you enrolled in the creative writing workshop?"

I had a sudden urge to flee. His eyes rested on every nanoparticle of my visible skin. I moved away a bit.

My smartphone continued to record.

"Lila," he said softly. "I have given this matter some thought, in fact a lot of thought. You found out, Lilawati, that my wife is taking that course. Later you made your father spend an entire day with us."

He was giving my detective ability more powers than it deserved. I had little idea about him and Lucia when I enrolled. Nothing more than a vague hunch. Perhaps some little things gleaned from magazines. But I didn't protest. I had an idea where he was going but also didn't know where he was going with all this, and I wanted him to go there without any interruptions.

Of course when my father spent the day with them it was not random. But I had not told my father anything complicated about Lucia and her family and I had not asked him to do anything for me. I had agreed to Lucia's offer because it would send a clear signal to Lucia's husband that I was not going to tell her anything about his affair, at least until we talked.

"In the spirit of clarification I would like to inform that I don't believe your father told you little. He is a loquacious man. Unlike you, he puts the other person at complete ease and one ends up making mistakes."

One ends up making mistakes—so he had thought about the coal mine, the slip-up, the lone survivor.

"What mistakes are you referring to?"

A long monologue ensued.

Vikram Jit paused for a while and turned his neck and stared at the homeless man for a long time.

The homeless man had on a grungy navy blue overcoat over his squarish body, a toque, loose blue jeans, scuffed brown boots, and an untamed beard. He was going through the foul-smelling bins. Unlike some other men in his situation he was not removing glass bottles, etc. He was different, it was clear, muttering things to himself.

I did interrupt Vikram Jit's monologues and his pauses. I must have felt safe enough; I even managed to say, "You never ceased to look like a ghost."

"I could say the same thing," he said, "about you, Lila."

■ ■ ■

Lila or Lilawati had no idea that she was going to die within the next few minutes. Fifty-one days ago she had encountered a woman called Lucia.

This story would have ended with Lilawati or Lila's death. But it did not. Because the woman called Lucia had also looked at a face from up close.

Lila was dead on the tracks. On the tracks, Lilawati's death was also Gauri's the second time. The police had problems keeping the curious crowd away. The homeless man was arrested. My backpack and the magazine were isolated with gloved hands for the forensic team to look at. Vikram Jit accompanied the cops to the station. He called Lucia to tell her to watch the evening news.

Lucia, not a regular watcher of TV, turned it on. She saw photos of me and the pigeon-saturated Sunnyside train station, low-resolution video footage of the homeless man. They didn't show the entire thing. Vikram Jit had walked up to the homeless man and said something to him. The homeless man grew angry. Vikram Jit is trying to calm him. Then the homeless man hits him and charges toward me. I am near the yellow line on the platform. A train is approaching, signals emit the usual ping, ping, ping, two sharp stabs of light, almost a blaze . . . Next thing I am on the tracks and the train takes care of me.

I am dead, but Lucia continues to think otherwise. She will continue this way for a while. She doesn't even have the option to call me. My cellphone is also on the tracks crushed into pieces. My body is still and still warm.

In my closed fist they find a small stone with a *Pikaia* fossil—Lucia's object.

The time is approximately 2 hours and 2.71828182845 90452353602874713527 minutes in the afternoon.

The TV channels show an interview with Vikram Jit, who is delivering the performance of a lifetime. Says I was interviewing him about his work on mitigating climate change. Says he has a high respect for me as a journalist. Claims the homeless man had made some violent gestures and he had gone to him to see if the man needed any help.

18

At first, I thought it was someone else. Then it dawned on me that the sound I was hearing was an echo of my own voice, words that came out of my own mouth and were delivered to my interlocutor only a few hours ago—

Something grand. Ambitious. Just the scale of it. It brings God and the transcendent back into the game. This is not a mere geologist making sense of some obscure fossils or moving them around. This is complete planetary redesign.

■ ■ ■

Not everyone was convinced. By the news. Of my departure.

Death is like that. It doesn't care whether we are convinced or not. It has its own logic. We can depart convincingly or unconvincingly. In the end it just doesn't matter. We can go heroically or brutally or tragically or accidentally or ridiculously; in the end it is the same thing.

One day we are alive, telling stories, alone or together, collaborators; one day we are all characters in each other's stories, and then we are dead.

One day we are giving birth to beauty and ugliness via stories, forming fresh bonds, breaking old ones, curious about ten thousand things and nothings.

'I am alive. I imagine the world before I was born. I imagine I was never born. I imagine myself dead. I imagine someone else dead. Someone else is alive. They imagine themselves dead. They imagine me dead. I am dead. They tell my story. I tell my story.'

One day we are telling stories in order to survive, and we survive in order to tell, and then, without any rhyme or algorithm it is "all over."

The dead know this better than the living. Because stories continue despite the discontinuities of migrations. Some of us get to stay alive to tell the story, and others must die to tell.

It is not the same thing, and yet it is the same thing. The main question, as always: Who is doing the telling?

I am, and I'll be quick. But before proceeding, I must, by way of a footnote, recap that stories always have the potential to become sublime and beautiful and geological like some transcendent ice sheet or a glacier, and one must never forget that the storyteller's authority is always "borrowed from death." That she herself is a small piece of ice core cut out of the same glacier.

■ ■ ■

Lila's photos appeared in all the papers the next day. *Calgary Herald. National Post. Globe and Mail.* The police were not discounting that some climate deniers had hired the homeless man to eliminate a bold journalist. Even right-wing tabloids published the photos and followed the story for several days. Lucia kept all the paper cuttings. She framed a black-and-white photo of me and hung it on a wall in her house. That was a difficult day for me because I thought the story terminated right there and then.

I could not have been more wrong.

Please ignore the last sentence. For now the only thing that matters is the fact that I was on the flame-orange wall, sharing it with other framed images.

On my left, Glenn Gould and Emily Carr. On my right, someone I didn't approve of, which saddened me, for I had unwittingly become the Canadian Emily Murphy's neighbour. Lucia knew only one aspect of Murphy, her involvement in the suffragette movement. She had little idea about Murphy's dark side, a constant supporter of eugenics until her last breath.

Maria Lassnig's *Two Ways of Being, Double Self-Portrait* (2000) and *Sprachgitter* (1999), right across from me, served as antidotes. Lucia had picked those reproductions from her mysterious Austrian neighbour's garage sale. *Two Ways of Being* almost brought me to tears. To counter intense emotions, I would silently stare at *Sprachgitter* (*Language Grid*) feverishly, hoping to take some of its algorithms, enigmatic voices, and prison bars for a long walk.

I don't want to judge or prescribe, but I liked it a lot when Lucia stepped out for a walk. Walks cheered her up authentically, reduced the need for medication (toxic multicoloured capsules, discs, even gummi bears). After a walk her face waved a caress toward all things big and small. I noticed a precarious habit of hers: she liked lighting scented candles, especially during the day. The burning candles, some fallen over, reminded me of Max Beckmann's *Still Life with Candles and Mirror* (1930). What a waste, I would almost murmur, fearing a spark from a smouldering candle could start a forest fire.

At home—a meticulously kept home—Lucia wore a strange cochineal jumper, one hundred years old, but it looked one thousand years old. At times I saw only her back—observing the old-fashioned barometer and thermometer hung outside the kitchen window. Now and then I called her "cochineal red jumper girl with a barometer."

On certain nights I felt like crying. But this is one thing the dead cannot do. Confusing at times, because Lucia doesn't cry either. Her "Anthropocene emotions" (and for that matter most emotions) were usually hard to read. My confusion deciphering her facial expressions cor- related well with the recent findings in neuroscience: *Our brains construct emotions. Our emotions are never culturally- linguistically-contextually independent.* Lucia had told me (at the museum) more about the everyday emotions she goes through, say, during a power blackout or when she sees a very old person recycling bottles. When her car warms up the seats (and buttocks) in winter. On certain days she feels like seeing and touching orchids over and over.

When I was alive, I so wanted to find out a scalpel-sharp word (in any language) for the way I felt when I would pick up ordinary objects and they would feel much warmer than they actually were. I wanted to figure the precise word for the complex emotions I used to go through looking at photos of poor female farmers hugging trees in Bangladesh, when printed collage-like next to the glossy photos of celebrity fashion models hugging trees in London. Emotions that filled me while reading about neologisms like "endling." An endling is "the last known individual of a species or a subspecies." The feeling that used to suffuse me when in contact with *indispensable* objects I desired, or when I raised the windows of my overheated room and kept them raised all through the night. My mood would fall whenever I thought about those friendly gender-reveal parties that set forests on fire. Or when I discovered that the grey flesh of a farmed salmon is dyed with canthaxanthin and astaxanthin to give it an edible "natural pink" look. Lucia had told me she felt a little shade of joy the moment she got rid of her picture postcard collection. I tried to do the same, and failed. At times, I, too, felt uncomfortable going to museums because museums failed to decolonize. The eco-grief I experienced was entangled with political disquiet: again and again the governments failed the Indigenous people even as some top leader issued spectacular apologies on behalf of the past. There were moments I simply could not face facts about my adopted country. Canada was one of the top three countries in the world when it came to per capita greenhouse gas emissions. Reading Shakespeare, Tagore or Atwood or any other classic was going to neither ease anxiety nor lower the emission numbers. Reading or writing fiction (and non-fiction) was only going to increase the heat, drown Bangladesh, then Bombay–Hamburg–New York, because to read and write books one requires (or still depends on) coal and oil . . . I would feel paralyzed . . . *Klimaangst* . . . Lucia had talked about emotional granularity . . . She did not know why she would fill up with hope despite all odds, and for days on end found no reason to doubt that favourite phrase of hers, "When the crisis is over."

Lucia and her husband were both collectors of objects. Lucia collected Guatemalan dolls, and her husband collected figurines of Ganesha. Haida Gwaii masks. Chacmool imitations. Soft spices . . . I loved the smell of bread baking . . . I imagined the smell whenever bread was baking . . . They ate different dishes whenever they ate dinner together. The children stapled on macaroni and cheese and rarely paid attention to blood oranges or to their mother cutting a juicy seed-saturated melon. With wet, sumptuous hands she skinned the melon with delightful hurry as if for a feast. Her husband was a pure dal-and-gobhi vegetarian who pretended there was no such thing as a sausage. She would chop a bit of parsley and he would chop a bit of coriander and no conflict ever gathered between their corianders and parsleys. In the mint-tiled bathroom she took short, cold showers; he liked them long and extra hot. She, averse to high heels indoors, walked barefoot with painted nails on wooden floors; he kept thin black or white socks on and whistled Bollywood tunes, and they never argued.

I had expected their relationship to be as imperfect as a gravel parking lot in some gentrifying part of the city, or a Netflix season, but it turned out to be a whole lot different. I had also imagined major irreconcilable differences.

The differences between them, as it became clear within a few days, were rather superficial, minor compared to a core similarity. Both made constant attempts to forget their respective pasts, and he, in my overall understanding, had been the more successful of the two, so successful that he had to borrow other people's stories and claim they were his own.

The kinds of things Lucia was trying to forget—or had already forgotten successfully—fell within the realm of guesswork. I knew so little about her, and on her own she had offered only a few details here and there. Of course we had just met, yet I have a feeling that she would not have shared much.

Their children knew more about Guatemala or Colombia than about Germany or India. I wondered how painful it would be for them when they started reading history, or felt its resuscitation.

■ ■ ■

Nine or so days later Lucia received a reminder call from the creative writing instructor. She had not submitted her novella on the German male nurse by the deadline. My name came up. Perhaps we should organize a memorial gathering, he suggested. She agreed and they reminisced about a few things.

"Why don't you come to my place?"

Lucia printed her manuscript. She was not happy with its progress despite having added handfuls of synecdoches, humour, and uncanny settings. She had followed the male nurse's trial keenly, but courtroom drama was the last thing she wanted to compose. Her physician had already increased her dose of antidepressant pills twice. The latest version of the manuscript began with laughter. Night laughter. The 678 dead patients are laughing at the nurse. The nurse is in solitary confinement. The prison—right next to a Neanderthal burial site. Through a sliver of a window, one could see hundreds of faintly illuminated wind turbines, turning and turning along. Lucia did some unnecessary editing. To please her principal reader she even managed to add quotations from *Macbeth*, especially from scenes that take place at night. Three hours later she reprinted the manuscript and carried it along.

The instructor lived near Chinatown in a newly built loft (orange coloured). She rang the bell twice. A woman dressed in Prada opened the door.

"Your next has come," she said to the instructor. Quickly she collected her Prada handbag and left.

Lucia had never seen this person at the workshop.

After making sure she was comfortably seated he volunteered the information himself.

"That young woman is a publicist for a local midsize publisher I know. She is brilliant, a raw intelligence. Trained in Toronto and New York."

The loft must have been next to the fire department; every now and then sounds of sirens wafted inside through glass walls.

He offered to make tea.

She settled for sparkling water.

"I had no idea Lila was a science journalist. When she came to me, she said she knew almost next to nothing about writing creatively."

Lucia wanted to say, "We were just beginning to know each other," but she ended up muttering, "I don't know, it doesn't feel real."

Both of them wanted to hug each other, but no such thing happened. Not long after, the main door opened on its own. One of the younger students I had seen hanging out with the instructor after the face workshop walked in and handed him a key.

"Sorry," she said.

"Sorry," he said. "I forgot."

"No, you didn't," she said. "I just came to return your keys and the front door fob."

"What do you mean?"

"It is over."

"Please give us a few minutes," the instructor said to Lucia and ran out of the door.

When an affair ends, one thinks about the last few days, what happened during the last few hours or moments the couple spent together. One must think instead about the first few days or the first few moments, things that were already there but never got acknowledged because to acknowledge them would have made it impossible to have the affair.

From where Lucia sat on an old patterned sofa, she could see a few indoor plants and one very long desk. Old photos and research and archival material connected to the history of oil and pipelines in the province of Alberta lay on the desk, also on the floor, basically spilling all over. Blocks of books, paper, and apparel. Sexy black-white-and-red-coloured T-shirts that said, "I heart oil and gas" and "I heart pipelines" and "Make coal great again." The instructor had stapled a couple of quotes from an Iranian journalist to the shoulder of one such T-shirt; the first one sounded as if the journalist belonged to some Gandhian civil disobedience movement. Lucia was impressed, however, by the second quote: "What if oil could speak? Is it already saying something to us?"

She had not studied the sciences, but she knew that the "dirty" oil that originates in Canada does not squirt up like Iranian oil. In her adopted country, huge volumes of steam were used to melt tar locked in sands hundreds of millions of years old; only then is it able to move. She wanted to use oil as a metaphor in her own novella-in-progress—melt it, make it flow.

In the loft she encountered bookshelves crowded with volumes on *Moby-Dick*, nature in Flaubertian novels, Shakespeare, and Finnish crime. There was a second desk. Lucia noticed a big pile of sheets on this desk. She walked closer, curious if I had submitted.

It didn't take her long to locate my manuscript. Double-sided. The instructor was taking his sweet time. After a brief moment of hesitation she transferred my work into her handbag on the old patterned sofa.

This was Lucia's one and only misstep in her work as a detective. I say misstep because her original intention was anything but glorious. She had relocated my manuscript to steal portions from my work.

She waited for the instructor for almost forty-five minutes, but there was no sign of him. So she scribbled a little note and shut the door and left. She didn't leave the printed version of her own work behind.

Back home she started reading my manuscript.

She was afraid the instructor would notice something missing. She did receive a collective email. He wanted to know if Lila had shared her manuscript with anyone. Or if anyone had seen it on his desk and taken it home by mistake. No one responded.

■ ■ ■

Lucia, it seemed to me right from the start, belonged to the class of people who are better readers than writers of texts. She was trained to read a text as if it were not connected to the real world at all. Some would say this approach has severe limitations for solving a serious crime. I have come to think otherwise.

Reading the text in this manner did not prevent her from visiting my apartment, and giving every inch of space a slow glance. Together with my father she went through the objects of the dead. My clothes, Gauri's kameez and cardigan. She found a large collection of black-and-white films from Japan; a hardbound collection of Chinese science fiction novels; complete works of my favourite author, Octavia E. Butler; twenty-two or twenty-three graphic novels from Bangladesh; a fat dictionary of Shakespeare (the instructor had asked us to "massage" our stories with quotes from *Hamlet*, *King Lear*, *Macbeth*, *Othello*, and *The Tempest*); an unread paperback by Anna Tsing, *The Mushroom at the End of the World: On the Possibility of Life in Capitalist Ruins*; a second-hand copy of *Silent Spring* by Rachel Carson; an ancient book on the Gond people and their myths, still in the brown package in which it was sent from one Michael Schama; and a five-page printout of email communication with a restless journalist friend of mine based in Darwin, Australia. Briefly a fly sat on the back of her hand. She shook it lightly, failed to get rid of the thing.

Erased of all data after three attempts at guessing the password, my laptop had been returned by the police. The hacker they hired had not found a single irregular file or folder. For some reason, forensics failed to return my belongings—a slim backpack (with Gauri's hand mirror) and a copy of the diasporic magazine.

Lucia watered the shrivelled plants on the balcony and sat in my empty chair and tried to make sense of the printout. The emails in question were an indirect way to get in touch with Dr. T, the Australian geologist whistle-blower. Like Dr. G, Dr. T, too, seemed to be avoiding me, and I'd contacted my Darwin colleague to persuade the forgotten hero to talk to me.

"Sorry, I've never heard of this guy. He doesn't seem to have a very heavy profile in CLIMATE. Thought you were keen on Charlie Veron, the barrier reef guy. Six scientists I am currently chasing for my own book ... So I am going to decline. I see your guy was caught up in outing a big name South Asian geologist over something some time ago. Maybe Dr. T doesn't wish to talk? Or maybe he is even dead. Email a colleague of Dr. T. Contact a 'geology department' colleague, saying you want to set up an interview to talk to them both (the main guy cc'd). This really gets the main guy going, I can tell you!!! Give it a go. Let me know how you go."

Lucia took off her heels. Her feet were hurting. She massaged a little and tiptoed to the washroom looking for a Band-Aid. Not far from the first-aid box there was a thing hard to ignore. It simply fell in her hands: a partially torn sheet of yellow legal pad paper, a sketch that made no sense at all. She almost damaged the sheet with her long fingernails.

Lucia applied the Band-Aid to her wounded toe and stared at my sketch (done with an HB pencil) for a long time. It was less a sketch, more an attempt to humour the researchers I had encountered at the climate lab, the ones who had interpreted my question about "a smartphone in an ice core" as a big "Earth after human extinction" question.

She did not know what it meant. My father did not know either.

Both of them laughed.

Lucia noticed moisture in his eyes.

Not having me in his life made him immensely alone. Death bites into our certainties. He would sit down on a chair in a dark room with an apple or a pear and make long Möbius strips, peeling them with a small knife. He seemed to have become a character in a black-and-white Japanese film by the director Yasujirō Ozu. Father must have imagined during younger years what would happen when he was no longer around. He must have feared certain bifurcating tomorrows: "What if my loved one goes before me?" The kind of conversation I never had with him was my exact reason for not marrying, for not having children.

He would not have understood if I had said climate change. I am quivering like a field of tall grass in the wind. My Anthropocene body's one major anxiety.

Lucia made my father chai without sugar. He slurped while drinking. The fly hovered around him like electric sparks. His dead daughter's friend drank bubbly water straight from the green bottle. Soon after, the bottle got discarded in the green recycling container. She felt good and made a serious attempt to bite a fingernail. She heard my voice then. She felt my voice was trying to mingle with her inner voice. She was going to find out more.

Neither one of them knew that with Annabel Sotto's help, I was in the process of conducting a "literary experiment" in the climate lab. The instructor had given us an assignment: "Compose two sci-fi stories, one set in the past and one in the future." My futuristic story was going to be narrated by an alien geologist, who manages to land on human-less Earth and discovers a smartphone in the debris of a lab. The alien gains access to memories and the complete mind of a single human being via the phone. Annabel did not see the point at first. She was a bit averse to the "mind uploading" genre. I insisted. So she allowed me "a little lab indulgence." By calling it "indulgence," she was in effect trying to buy my silence about the conference hotel incident. She allowed me to plant a live smartphone (designed for extreme conditions; non-lithium batteries) in a simulated ice core cylinder at $-36°C$. If the phone continued to work, it could also be synched with my regular smartphone, the one I carried in my pocket all the time. In short, when I was secretly recording Amitabh Ghosh at the Sunnyside train station, the recording was also being stored simultaneously in the climate lab.

■ ■ ■

A few days after my death Annabel Sotto thought of removing the device from the cylinder. She could not find it. She double-checked the lab book. All locations clearly marked.

She knew I could not have altered or removed it from the spot where it had been originally placed. To add or remove things one required special access.

She checked with men who had been given temporary access to the facility to fix the heat removal, i.e., the cooling system. She sent a memo to everyone in the lab. No one knew how that object had disappeared.

Nothing had been overtly vandalized.

Dr. Kimeu conducted his own little investigation, slow and thorough, but nothing came of it. Highly disoriented, he stepped out of the lab and sat down on a gneiss rock under a deciduous tree. Thinking-man pose. Before his mind moved to some major channels, he thought about me for a split second and smiled. He thought about our one and only pub conversation. I had gone to Moxie's with him to indirectly find out a few things about Sotto and Ghosh, but he had changed the channel and confessed something personal. "Three years ago I told a lie to someone I care about a lot." When he found out that his wife was having an affair, he told her that he, too, was having an affair. Everything about his affair was imaginary. He asked for forgiveness. She did the same. Both of them forgave each other. "Who does the imaginary woman look like?" I had asked. He had smiled.

■ ■ ■

I really wanted Dr. Kimeu to connect with Lucia.

One night Lucia looked at the lobes of her ears in a mirror and realized she had not made love for several months. She initiated the process clumsily on the queen-size bed with freshly washed and ironed sheets, and her husband responded. He was ungentle with her breasts. There was a curious distance between them. The TV was still on. During the motions she wiggled her toes and crumpled and sheared and crushed a pillow; she must have been trying to recall me then or trying to forget me, because right after, she started asking him about geology.

She used to ask him such questions when they had just met. What is geology? she asked him again.

"Compilation of one ruin after another," he said. "What seems so sublime and beautiful to our imagination now is simply the persistence of what vanished a while ago."

"What is a while ago?"

He made waves with an index finger in air as if plotting a graph of *deep time*.

She showed him my sketch then. What does this mean?

During that vulnerable moment he made a mistake, something he regretted right after. Still on the bed, half-naked, his hand reached out for the reading glasses on the side table. Within seconds he was encouraging his wife to go visit the ice core lab at the university, as if this matter was not connected at all to the matter brewing in his mind.

■ ■ ■

That night at Moxie's Dr. Kimeu had just ordered beer when a familiar voice invaded by way of an apology.

"Sorry."

"No, no, we are interruptible."

Annabel Sotto brought a strange mood to our pub table, extremely quiet at first. She stared at my face in dim refracted light. She was wearing expensive clothes and sharp earrings and asked me a couple of inoffensive questions about India. From then on, we were all over the place. Later, when the old scientist beckoned the waiter, I, too, thought of calling it a night. Annabel insisted we hang out a bit longer; she ordered a bottle of Rioja. After the second glass she told me stuff I did not want to go near. Something that originally came out of Ghosh's mouth.

When in high school in Red Deer, Alberta, the newly arrived immigrant Lucia met a fellow called Jimmy. Jimmy was her age, unmuscular but handsome, and simply took her breath away. One day he said he was ready to take the relationship to the next level. Jimmy had it all planned out. "We meet my parents at the Joe's Grill this evening."

What transpired at the bar-restaurant took wings out of Lucia. Jimmy's smartly dressed father arrived a full forty-five minutes late. He looked as if the ship of his life had left without him. Lucia heard him say, "Your mom will follow shortly."

Jimmy had a little chat with Dad about the brand new Malibu Wakesetter boat. "Possible to borrow it, Dad? Lucia and I are headed to Lake Invermere." They ordered sparkling water, wine, and meaty herb-garnished food; Jimmy kept telling the waitress with silver hair that one more person was going to join the table.

While drinking the second bottle of wine— Argentinian Merlot or Malbec—and eating the main course of pink and medium-well-done steak, Jimmy's father grew a bit agitated. "I think your mom has left me." The two youngsters thought it was a joke and laughed. But when the mom did not show up at all, Jimmy's father said in a terrible voice, "Perhaps I did something to her." And the two youngsters asked in unison, "What do you mean?"

Later the police found Jimmy's mom dead in the house, and his father confessed without making any further trouble that they had had an argument, and he had used a carbon fibre ski from the garage to scare her a bit.

Two days later Jimmy attempted suicide. With the wheel of a can opener. Emergency rushed him to a hospital and admitted him to a special ward where he died of a heart attack. The doctor on duty tried four or five times, perhaps seven or eight times, but failed to revive his heart.

When Annabel took a cab from the pub that night, I walked home all alone thinking about the near-endless task of fishing out story traces from the past lives of a single human being, someone much cared for. We find patterns, connections we did not see before, but new questions, new doubts emerge and take us back—or we stumble—into the familiar-unfamiliar ocean. With slightly bigger fishing nets.

■ ■ ■

Annabel, visibly puzzled when Lucia walked into her office, could not utter a single word. Lucia had not phoned or emailed in advance, but she did not understand why the climate scientist was so startled when she knocked on the office door.

She just wanted to show the director a found sketch. Consult about enigmatic markings. Locate meaning. Even a trace of a meaning would do. By now she had made several photocopies, as if she was soon going to post them all over the city in order to locate a lost gnome or a cat.

Annabel's breath was restored the moment she looked at the sketch. She did not know how to tell Lucia what had already transpired in the lab.

"When did you get this diagram?"

"Just told you," said Lucia. "I had no idea it existed before Lila's passing."

"What do you think this is?"

The way Lucia shook her head conveyed next to nothing.

"What do you think?"

"My husband said only this lab could decipher such things."

Dr. Sotto, in the middle of an analysis, did not feel like sending Lucia away. She became overly kind toward the stranger. The kind of kindness that comes from guilt-induced perturbations.

"Come back in forty-five minutes," she said. "I will try my best to help."

Lucia spent some time wandering through the sprawling university campus. Some young people, a diverse group, were demonstrating; the whole thing had the feel of civil disobedience. But one of them, in a hoodie, standing a bit apart, was paying more attention to trees. Elm trees. Nearly thirty years ago, in 1989, fourteen trees were planted in memory of fourteen female Canadian scientists and engineers murdered by a white male mechanical engineering student. The young woman stared at Lucia's face, but Lucia did not see it.

When she returned Dr. Sotto lent her a green polar jacket and a merino wool toque, and together they walked into the ice core lab. The director, together with grad students and post-docs, conducted a thorough search yet again. The excess of lights they turned on flooded the near-uncountable cylinders. Lucia's lipstick glistened.

They located the phone.

More mysterious than the disappearance was the reappearance. Reappearance (upside down) in a different ice cylinder, with an entirely different label.

Dr. Sotto tried to turn it on in Lucia's presence. The phone was as good as dead, like its mortal shadow on the floor, and remained so when no longer frigid, a mystery she would not resolve that day, not even with the help of super-elegant problem-resolving infectiously joyous mildly plump IT experts.

Lucia took off her borrowed toque. The toque suited her, but no one told her that. Soon the cobbled streets by the climate lab swelled up with sounds of people getting into their cars.

■ ■ ■

The most relevant part of Lila's conversation with Vikram Jit at the open-air Sunnyside train station continues to stay with me. "Stay" is not the right word; it sounds like "trapped within me." Let me revise. The conversation is embodied in my new way of being, the kind of embodiment that helps clear up things. Here, I, Lila, present a few traces and echoes of the lost recording.

The dead man: "You used to be brilliant in the lab, Lilawati, and yet, and yet you always scored low on theory. You fumbled. The key stuff remained beyond your grasp. As always there are traces of a sheer genius in that head over shoulders. But, deep down, you also are a fragile creature who envies theorists. You want to clear up things. But you forget I, too, want to clear them up. Let us do a thought experiment, you and I, let us try to bring all your diagrams to the table. In your situation, with your low aptitude for logical thinking and tendency to rely on rumours, I would have come up with more or less the same diagrams about our mutual friend. You are absolutely sure Gauri did not jump on her own. I am with you there; she did not jump on her own, nor am I protecting her. It is the rest of your conjecture I disagree with. You believe Gauri found out a few things, hidden or concealed, she should not have—just before the field trip. You believe she was just about to become some grand unsung heroine of a whistle-blower. You also wrongly believe that I said something to the madwoman on the train; in effect, I made her push Gauri out of the train. At times you believe it was I who pushed your friend. All this, too easy, too simple to imagine. Truth is far more subtle than this, far more inconvenient. Let us step back and think about other possibilities. That what happened to Gauri was genuinely an accident. She could have been worried about me. Perhaps I knew or found out something. Perhaps I witnessed the hit-and-run murder of the lab assistant. You have even imagined the worst. That I took the money and murdered Professor G's man. But at the end of the day this is just a good thought experiment. Thing is, after Gauri's accident I fled not because I took away someone's life, but in order to save my life."

The living woman: "The lab technician knew about your little discoveries as well."

The dead man: "It would have been good had it all come out then. I was a student. All of a sudden, everyone was blaming everything wrong in the department on the disgraced man. I would have perhaps done the same. I deserved a better teacher. We all did. We are all his collateral damage. I am in accord with you here. During so

many sleepless nights I still think about the PhD supervisor who gave birth to G . . . but I don't know where to
stop. Stop with G's teacher or with G's teacher's teacher?
I know what you are thinking now. Why didn't I come
clean ten or fifteen years ago? Because as time passed, it
became more and more difficult. I had changed my name.
So it became even more difficult. Lucia did not know
about any of this. So it became more and more difficult."

The living woman: "Not difficult. But impossible.
Because you are dead."

The dead man: "I am both dead and alive. You know
I am involved with two immensely important planetary life-saving projects right now. Any association with
Professor G, etc., will not bode well for the project or
funding. It will create doubt. I don't ask you to do anything special for me. I only request you think about all
this carefully before you make any decision."

The living woman: "I cannot stop thinking about
Gauri and I cannot stop thinking about the murdered
lab technician."

It was at this point Vikram Jit walked toward the
homeless man.

19

This is perhaps the shortest chapter I will ever write. Short, with enormous speed and smell of irony. Ironic, because this chapter is about long hours and slowness in real life, and serious, careful noticing.

After the IT experts gave up, Annabel Sotto took home the HD surveillance videos they had left behind. She watched the footage with patience normally reserved for fieldwork in Antarctica and Greenland. Weeks of footage. Several times her left hand rewound and froze images. She flagged one person, a university insider. She could not understand why he had accessed the climate lab (not once but thrice). The footage revealed only entries and exits; there was no record of what someone did inside the lab. The suspect was a professor of petro-geology; she knew he was a highly social guy, who ran full marathons every summer and did heli-skiing every winter.

She emailed the professor right away and arranged to meet in his office, which was in a different building, first thing in the morning.

"I was given access to the lab by the previous director," he explained. "This term I am teaching Petroleum 101. While covering the chapter on drilling technologies, I thought the class would be thrilled to discover a remarkable paradox—the significant role played by petro-geologists when it comes to collecting some of the most precious data connected to climate change. Without our drilling techniques there would be no ice cores—"

Annabel Sotto was listening. But she only wanted to find out one thing.

"By any chance did you remove something from the lab?"

■ ■ ■

"We borrowed a couple of cylinders. I ought to have left a little note. Sorry, the last few months have been a bit rushed. We only borrowed the simulated ice core cylinders. Not the real thing."

"Were the students allowed to come in contact with the cylinders?"

"The class was curious. They had permission to use hands. Minimal, I would say."

Annabel Sotto allowed the pause to grow longer than usual.

"Any guest lecturers involved in this course?"

"Why do you ask?"

"Pure curiosity."

"One of our finest," he said, maintaining the same serious look on his face. "Dr. A. Ghosh."

20

I read somewhere that a poet finished her poem—four stanzas—in five years. Between the first word and the last there were five long or short years. Time, at times, is no more than a number.

One night in the bedroom I witnessed Lucia inform her husband that Lila's unfinished book would soon see the light of the day. Graced by a gorgeous and arresting green-and-purple cover (suffragette colours), the novella was also going to carry a short, heartfelt note by the instructor of the writing workshop. The publisher (who spoke like a used-car salesman) was a friend of the instructor and a diehard supporter of texts unaccompanied by their authors. Everyone in the workshop, barring one, promised to promote the book. Lucia was also going to be associated with all the press releases on my behalf.

"Is it a novel?" asked Lucia's husband.

"Yes, a novel."

"A work of fiction?"

"A novel is always a work of fiction."

"Did Lila write something indecent?"

"Such things depend on the reader."

■ ■ ■

At this point I thought, So this is how the story ends, with the publication of my work. Nothing gets resolved fully. I must confess my soft spot is for narrations that don't end with a dot. I like them to end with a drop—a little drop of limpid water that falls on an absorbent sheet of paper; slowly it keeps advancing the liquid-air interface, making the *wet circle* bigger and bigger.

Lucia and the workshop instructor moved several passages around, even erasing the opening paragraph— the one I wrote before anything else.

Often, I wake up in the middle of the night as if the person closest to me just revealed that everything they told me about their past was a lie.

There are seven kinds of liars.

You are one of them.

I, as a writer of fictions, am definitely one of them. Fiction is not a lie that reveals truth. Fiction—as someone said—is a falsehood that reveals falsehoods.

21

In my book, the original book I wrote, the book not yet edited by Lucia (the one you may never get to read), I killed Amitabh Ghosh.

In the original I became a thing, the thing that sent the husband to the stratosphere.

Lucia changed the ending. I had done no such thing in real life, but she and the instructor didn't like that I had killed a man in the story. The man in the story, the one I had written, was not the real Amitabh Ghosh; he was simply some aspects, some semblances of Amitabh Ghosh, but it made her uncomfortable to read him dead, so they resurrected him, let him live, and it ruined the effect.

■ ■ ■

The book did not have a long shelf life. Eighty-two copies sold the first month, and the following month, two copies at half price. Lucia read a few passages from the middle chapters at three or four public events.

She especially chose those passages in which the narrator's voice mixes Earth time and human time. She would end the public readings sharing a strange anecdote. The anecdote would expand like bread in an oven and get nibbled at during wine and cheese. *Only a few weeks before Lila ended up on the tracks, I had asked her if it was fate, chance, or choice that brought us together. Lila closed her eyes and took a deep breath. All of the above, she said, and none. She smiled. But she grew silent. Do you really want to know? she asked suddenly. We would never have met if our world lacked cheap fossil fuels. Her thoughts touched me and left me speechless, as always.*

Michael, the used-bookstore man, was present during one of her readings. The seat on his left was conspicuously empty, but the seat on his right was occupied by a person who resembles a Delhi-based cousin of mine.

The workshop instructor did a jumpy radio interview, perhaps two, and said nice things about me, although I must confess one phrase of his was plain wrong. "The beauty of books like this," he said, "will *cure* the Anthropocene." He had no idea what he was talking about. But he managed to rescue the situation. He read from an old email of mine thanking him for the "face-observing" activity; he said the real thanks should go to a group in Poland that uses the technique to create closeness between natives and refugees. Other than that a few online reviews appeared, and then the book and its author were forgotten.

Even Lucia had forgotten me. She grew tired, as expected.

The living are always a bit afraid that they will forget the dead. By the time they actually forget, they no longer recall the fear. By this time they have figured out techniques to live comfortably without any interaction with the dead.

What hurt me more than anything else was that Lucia had forgotten making many other "minor" changes in my one and only book. I knew she would never allow me to kill her husband, but why continue to make more and more changes, as if the book were really hers? This I still don't comprehend. One particular edit of hers brought about a strong response within me, an emotion I had never experienced before. I cannot rely on a single proper word for that emotion or feeling in all the five languages I know.

Was it Lucia or my instructor who cut out a mildly lyrical, breathless (paragraph-less) passage of mine five or six pages long? The one done in italics. Something intimate and personal: a large part of the passage was based on a childhood memory of a cyclone of a superstorm in India.

Now I know many things, but some things of essence, her things, her decisions, still elude me. What made Lucia change her original intention? Why did she not steal from my work? Her revised intention escapes me as well. She decided to edit my work (heavily) instead.

■ ■ ■

The following passages—intimate truths of a lived life—found themselves deleted as well:

I was walking up the slopes of a mountain (Sleeping Buffalo) in the Rockies. The air was crisp, and even the soft needles of larches were turning sulphur yellow. Suddenly a huge elk appeared. Right in front of me, a mother with two children. One by one they grew absolutely still, staring. I was warned to take cover in such situations. Harsh bugle-like rutting sounds could be heard now coming from somewhere close. This was most likely a male elk, fully antlered. I almost took a step back, but in the end remained glued to my spot.

Thus began an unusual face-to-face staring exercise. The mother elk's eyes saw better than mine; I knew I was both a danger to them and in danger myself. She moved her head slightly. A nimble movement brought it back to the original position.

We continued staring. Three or four minutes passed. Only when I heard the rutting sounds again did I feel a sense of urgency and change my path. If I had not changed my path, I would not have encountered S.

S stood in front of a log cabin.

S was very different from me, yet at that moment I only saw S as a member of the human species. This melting of our differences lasted for a couple of minutes only, but during those couple of minutes I kept thinking about my face-to-face with the elk. During those three or four minutes I was clearly aware that I belonged to a strange species and simultaneously aware in a transcendental way that the elk and I both belonged to "lifeness" on Earth (and not Mars or Venus). I knew this kind of staring would not work with a tiger or a virus or bacteria, but it was working with wild ungulates, with that particular elk. On both sides there was no fear. I will never know what exactly went through the elk, the wapiti, but a little bond was formed. Trust was established. The children, too, were curious, even more than the mother, and felt safe enough to turn to grass and grazing while the staring was going on.

Those three or four minutes are the closest I have ever come to an experience that can only be called multi-scalar. Sort of metaphysical. Cognitively I am aware of such stuff, but one is not talking cognition. It was such a short duration, but I can go on reflecting about the duration forever.

■ ■ ■

Let's talk about hope, S said in front of the log cabin. Hope is my vocation, I said cautiously. But I only practise it when there is no hope left.

Hope lies in sulphur, S said.

"Sulphur, the English word, comes from shulbari in Sanskrit," I said. "It is highly reactive, eats anything it comes in contact with more or less the same way it eats copper." (Shulba = copper; ari = enemy.)

"This means we won," S said.

"We lost. Shulbari won."

Over and over I try to persuade Lucia: revert faithfully to the original. But she refuses to listen.

Over and over I try to explain: S is an imagined character, a composite. S doesn't stand in for her husband.

Another deleted portion of the manuscript. In this passage the narrator floats about in the stratosphere, twelve to fifty kilometres above sea level, trying to block the sun. It is hot up there. Left and right have lost their usual meaning. I am wearing dark glasses, a supernal suit; my face is a burning yellow smile. Most sulphur around me is in the form of highly reflective spheres, 0.1-micron body diameter, perfect for shielding the sun.

I had composed the science fiction passage the day I found an albino cockroach in my glass of water. It felt unreal. Cockroaches in a Canadian city. I blew it out of the window and resumed writing. The cockroach made me think of a verse in the Gita, the one Oppenheimer had recited after detonating the nuclear weapon.

Now I am become Death, the destroyer of worlds.

A few paragraphs later:

Then I was Myth, a Goddess, a glowing Sita, a Parvati, a Cassandra, a Draupadi. I saw global warming being reversed. The planetary cooling was quick and cheap and the process exceptionally simple.

I witnessed the final solution: thousands of helium balloons attached to hoses morphed into designer volcanoes, injecting colloids into the stratosphere. Marine stratocumulus clouds brightened themselves into giant mirrors. Sacks of iron sulphate fertilized the oceans. Soils grew a reflective skin, enhancing Earth's albedo.

Artificial-intelligence algorithms made decisions about who was to live and who the next sacrifice.

There they were, Krishna and Zeus, going rogue, Engineers going ironic, using Earth systems science as an alibi.

In the epoch of tantalum and hyperobjects and tipping points, I saw techno-managers dissolving old troubles by precipitating implacable new ones, I saw most life on Spaceship (Earth) voluntarily or involuntarily playing the role of the dog Laika.

Now I am become Saviour, the preserver of worlds.

"Manage the sun: our only option," the managers were saying.

We will fix it, they said as if a chorus.

We will shrink the asteroid and provide solid proof that the Anthropocene was good, a stepping stone for our evolution as a species. Our intelligence will conjoin and colonize the whole cosmos.

We melted the hands of the Doomsday Clock. Other flawed ideas broke—on their own—like pottery. Earth After Us was a mere fantasy in the collective unconscious. We displayed its counterfactuals in museums by the sea. Already we live in the stable era—a.k.a. the Novacene.

We can create an ice age on demand or make our planet as hot as Venus. We can kill life, and then we can resuscitate life, we can manage life. We can edit Natural Selection. Ourselves. With enormous speed. We are special on this planet because of speed. Take away speed and we are nothing.

We must learn to love our monsters. We must acknowledge that technology is never ideal, they said. We knew, from the start, that our sun-dimming bodies would not be able to maintain the 0.1-micron diameter. Possible coalescence and sedimentation of small SO_2 spheres were not unknown. We predicted and worried about possible weakening of monsoons in Asia, high hydrological stresses, disruption of food chains, new *types of wars erupting between India and China, mass starvation, pandemics, geoterrorism.*

We worried about termination shock. (I.e., catastrophes caused by dangerous temperature rise as a result of prematurely stopping the sulphur injections in the stratosphere. We were aware that once started we could not afford to stop the injections in fifty years, not even a hundred years; we knew we had to go on for a minimum of a thousand years.)

We expected the unexpected, but not this kind of unexpected . . . the managers were saying.

I wrote more:

Now I am Sita, a Parvati, a Cassandra, a Draupadi, a timid goddess, I witnessed the end of world-without-end. Collapse of one species after another, with uncanny spatial variations. End of sapiens in Africa, where they originated. New York covered in barium fog. Truth sandwiched between layers of rock. I participated in grand pyrrhic victories won by the rich nations, and realized that there was no need now to recite beautiful myths and tales about parents who kill their own children. We were those parents and Gretel and her brother Hansel never came back.

■ ■ ■

When she woke up, capitalism was still there.

■ ■ ■

When she woke up, anthropocentrism was still there.

■ ■ ■

She woke up thinking, "When I stare at the acknowledged and unacknowledged human suffering, I seem to
forget the planetary. When I seriously notice the planetary things, I seem to forget human suffering. How shall I
integrate the two without erasing one or the other?"

■ ■ ■

When I woke up, almost a year later, April the 23rd, I
remembered that it was actually my birthday. What does
"when I woke up" mean when one no longer opens and
shuts one's eyes? Sleep has a different meaning for me
now. Night has a fresh meaning. The living go to sleep to
escape the real. They wake up to escape the dream. I no
longer operate within the loops of escape. I can endure
both the real and the unreal. My new way of being is not
without its comforts.

Lucia baked a near perfection of a plum cake. Not
because she remembered (you cannot celebrate a birthday—my birthday—the one that never registered in
your mind). She went through the trouble because of a
deep love for baking, and at least two of her children
would eat it.

April 23rd was also the birthday of a wayward teenage boy in India. Padma, his larger-than-life mother,
baked a layered coconut cake knowing full well that her
son would not even touch it. Mother and son were not on

speaking terms. Padma took the cake in a tiffin to work. During a seminar she shared it with colleagues. She distributed fat wedges on disposable plates. The colleagues wished her luck during tea; she was flying abroad the following Monday to attend a conference on geology.

■ ■ ■

For me Padma was a distant memory. When we were young no fondness or affection trapped us with bonds. Under different circumstances the trajectories we followed after finishing the Chandigarh undergrad program might not have intersected.

For now this is the situation. Padma flew out of Lucknow in India to Morocco, not knowing that during her presentation at the conference she would not be able to answer properly a simple question. Five days later she returned home, embarrassed and humiliated, and could not help but look at Dr. G's papers. Especially at the names and institutions of all of G's co-authors.

All this occurred around the time of publication of my novella. Padma, unaware, somewhat out of the loop, had no idea that I had become an author. She found out indirectly from Amrit, the assistant professor in Chandigarh. Padma—the selfsame mysterious student in my university geology class, the one who kept her hair in braids, the one who was bitten by a street dog, the one who nearly lost an eye, the one who was Ruby or Vikram Jit's lab partner for a while.

I used to find her odd; everyone in our class did. Even our juniors (people like Amrit) reached the same conclusion. Padma never read any poetry or novels and was proud of this limitation. "Stories obfuscate." She couldn't comprehend why painters don't label their works properly. So if a visual artist sketched a horse, she wanted the artist to tell the viewer unambiguously what kind of horse it was. It was not enough to paint a tapeworm or a sperm whale; artists must identify the exact type of sperm whale and provide details of its normal habitat. She was at once odd and awkward, a good student despite her oddities.

Regarding Padma in the present (less youthful looking than me), it would be helpful to take a quick look at two things in particular.

The first one concerns something rather personal. Personal unhappiness and worries. Her teenage son, "a sweet kid," fell from grace. Someone who rarely used the word *fuck* growing up fell into the oil well of wrong company. Extreme-right, neo-fascist variety of radicalization. Padma blamed the schools, recent changes made to history. The new textbooks peddled myths and fantasy and colonial narratives about "Hinduism" adopted by upper-caste Hindu supremacists. If she had managed to instill a certain scientific attitude, he dumped it by the roadside. Obviously, the boy was rebelling against Padma and her husband; all teenagers go through a surreal phase. What worried her was her son's inclement U-turn and rejection of "critical thinking," his sudden obedience to "alternative facts" and taking orders from the Great Leader, who claimed ancient

Indians practised science more advanced than modern science. Vedic Indians knew genetics, stem cell research, organ transplant; they knew how to land a craft on Jupiter and foolproof geoengineering. The Great Leader (someone the Nazis would have sent to a gas chamber) didn't confine himself to fantasy about the past; he had modified India with "Hindu" architectures and called the minorities in the country rats and termites, and so had Padma's son.

No idea if she knew that her son frequented dimly lit bars and hung out with digital thugs who abused female journalists on WhatsApp, Facebook, and Twitter. Together they made fake videos of independent-minded journalists performing pornographic acts.

While in Morocco, Padma's heart accelerated in the four-star hotel room. How anti-knowledge had civil society become? Her teenage son really believed crap like "Cow dung cures viral contamination, and ends plagues and famines." "No one has seen a monkey turn into a man, so Darwin was dumb." "Hindu fire yagna religious ritual will clean the air pollution." "Aryans—pure-race—originated in India and built the Harappan civilization where Brahmans manipulated human DNA with CRISPR." "Lord Brahma discovered dinosaurs," according to a non-ironic paper presented by a Panjab University geology professor at the 2019 Indian Science Congress. "Climate change is a hundred percent *natural* process," according to a Panjab University alumnus who studies melting glaciers in the Himalayas; most likely he took a course on "global warming" from Professor G decades ago.

The second thing was connected to G's papers. G's best-known papers—those published in *Nature*—were all co-authored with highly respected names in geology. In fact it had to do with the long list of spectacular G co-authors who were never brought to any trial, not even a show trial by some global body of science. One hundred and seventeen in total, more than half of them from outside of India, especially in the West.

There is a third thing as well. Padma's internationally recognized work on vertebrate fossils.

In Morocco a distinguished colleague made a serious accusation against her earlier work, a paper that involved invertebrates. Something published during her student days in Chandigarh. "Cargo-cult science." The accuser directed this provocative phrase at her, a slap in the face.

"For some strange reason," he continued, "I cannot locate your co-author."

"My co-author is dead."

Padma was a bit defensive at the conference. She felt humiliated and wanted to clear her name. She took a break from research and teaching and revisited not only her own paper from some other era but also all the irregular papers she could get her hands on.

Dr. Padma Jangarh Shyam, the Indian colleagues knew, had done some of her best work either in the field, where she studied rare dinosaur nesting sites and eggs (in Western India), or in her study. She was part of a team that saved rare dinosaur fossils from being destroyed by a cement factory. Her team had also received praise from some international peers, as it had reproblematized a major question. The question took us back in time: some sixty-six million years ago when more than sixty-six percent of plant and animal species were wiped off the face of the Earth. A Delhi-based science reporter described the ongoing (vigorously debated) work as follows: *In addition to the asteroid (that fell near Yucatán, Mexico), it is now becoming increasingly clear that deep-time India might be "implicated" in the extinction of dinosaurs! Some 400,000 years before the asteroid fell, a massive volcano erupted in India. The lava flows were like an oceanic river almost the size of the entire subcontinent, and buried India under 11,000 feet of basalt rock. The eruption could have perturbed the planetary climate systems, triggering a warming phase and the weakening of the biosphere. Some international scientists have come to the conclusion that India was solely responsible for the mass extinction of dinosaurs, that the end-Cretaceous mass extinction was going to happen anyways (even if the asteroid didn't fall on Earth). However, Dr. Padma J. Shyam's team has come to a different conclusion. The team doesn't deny volcanism in India, it happened "beyond reasonable doubt"; the team doesn't disagree that India's Deccan Traps released huge pulses of CO_2 in the atmosphere. However, the team's work suggests that the dinosaurs might have survived if the asteroid had failed to fall on Earth. "Let us not forget a tiny alga." Tiny calcareous algae (in huge amounts) might have absorbed colossal amounts of CO_2 from the atmosphere and saved not just T. rex (and Zuul), but their* Indian cousins as well—Rajasaurus, Indosaurus, Titanosaurus, Laevisuchus, Isisaurus, *and* Jainosaurus.

And if the dinosaurs had survived, I would not be writing this article, and you would not be reading it, or listening to it while driving around.

■ ■ ■

She lived in a modest apartment by the edge of the city. When working from home (the colleagues did not know) Padma was unusually creative when barefoot or sitting on a carpet. For this reason not a single desk or settee, nor an IKEA chair, graced her study. A spare, low-entropy study.

On one of the whitewashed walls there was a large-format handwritten quotation done in an HB pencil:

The earth was diminishing as the earthworm
was eating it slowly.
—GOND creation myth

Usually she didn't go near myths, but this one line she liked because of an Earth sciences connection. Once in a while she shared the quote with an eager international scientist. She was fully aware of its power; for instance, the line always turned a conversation toward the Indian origin of an important word in geology: *Gondwana. Forest of the Gonds.*

If the foreign colleague was likeable, by way of a digression she would volunteer stuff about the Gond people and their remarkable walking pilgrimages. "To Gonds, the Narmada River is more sacred than the Ganga. Every year they circle the entire river at least once (some 2,600 kilometres long), always keeping the water toward their right. Most walk barefoot, the best way, the most primal, the most radical and joyous way to walk." After the digression she would speak her mind about the "human" and the new word.

> "There is no such thing as the Anthropocene," she would say. "There are Anthropocenes."
> "What exactly do you mean?"
> "We have Anthropo-seens and Anthropo-unseens."
> "Meaning?"
> "For some Anthropocene is all crime and little punishment. For others it is little crime and all punishment."

Padma opened all the windows of her apartment, took off her red socks, walked into the study and sat cross-legged examining a visual shock of an image in a large-format book. The artist had imagined the creature responsible for leaving behind conodont tooth fossils (Dr. G's enigmatic conodonts). "What is the conodont saying to me? If only I could listen."

She was staring at lily-like crinoids and *Fusulinida forams. Graptolithina* (Greek—*graptos*, written; *lithos*, rock). She could not tear herself apart from those enigmatic markings. Were they true fossils? Were they *pictures resembling fossils*? "If only I could listen."

Padma nearly felt my presence then. She reasoned the room was noisy because of rustling of paper.

Overpowered by a sudden urge (and maintaining my distance) I lay down on the carpet. The light was still unstable, and for a while I found myself behaving as if Padma were completely absent from the room. Even her penetrating gaze produced no effect within me.

There I lay on my back for a long time. Sinking more and more into Mother Earth.

Opening my eyes I found Padma not far from me in the same shavasana posture on the same carpet.

She reflected about co-authors in general. How fragile that relationship is. Something based on mutual trust and pure ambition. Both parties stand to make enormous gains, real and perceived. The same G who was involved with the lab technician's murder was also a wizard of writing scientific papers—the type of magic science doesn't celebrate after fall from grace. What was his method?

Padma, curious with every breath, found a partial answer in a little book. G would approach a distinguished or rising star of a scientist. Look, I just found this fossil in the Himalayas. Would you like to write a paper together? The distinguished or rising star would agree right away with saliva in mouth. G's fossils were no ordinary things; he always "found" the ones used to mark geological time. This person would then write the entire paper based on sketchy and flawed data.

After Dr. T exposed stolen and misplaced fossils, misplaced images of fossils, etc., most co-authors abandoned G. The way rats abandon a sinking ship. No one wanted to share blame. Perhaps they were parrots, and not rats. Perhaps they were a wolverine, an otter, a lynx, a muskrat, a grizzly, a beaver, a rhino, a weasel, an ant. Each co-author must have a unique story to tell. Only a handful came forward, and whatever was told remains scattered and is getting ready to vanish into oblivion.

But where does Vikram Jit fit into all this?

Padma was sweating heavily on the carpet and there was nothing I could do to wipe it away.

■ ■ ■

It was around then a colleague gave her my novella (with French flaps). Padma read it slowly the first time, and slowly the second time. It was the first fictional text she had read in her life. Most likely the last. She read it as if a work of non-fiction. Every single line in the book (just like the author's biography) seemed to be connected to the world outside the book. As soon as she finished, she knew she had to contact Lucia (who was promoting Lila's work) and applied for a Canada visa.

I hear someone breathing. Who? During the first portion of her long flight, from Delhi to Toronto, she found herself sitting not far from a bunch of European men as noisy as fishmongers, who kept saying "We are semen." They were seamen, and this is how they pro-nounced the word. She could not control her smile at this linguistic misunderstanding. At this point in time she had no idea that the smartly dressed Punjabi woman (from Delhi) sitting next to her was headed to locate a man who had vanished. The woman soon after showed Padma a big, fat wedding photo. An IT man had married her, promising a permanent move to Canada, only to disappear a week later. Padma had no idea how to help this sufferer who spoke little English. She wished her luck at the Toronto airport, the young woman took a connecting flight to Vancouver, and Padma flew onward to Calgary.

Padma had also carried a photo during that flight. On the night of her arrival she got locked out of the Airbnb house (next to an abandoned car-wash station). She spent an hour in the chill watching feral rabbits. The rabbits froze stiff when lights from a garbage truck fell on them, and pneumatic sounds nipped through discarded materials and faintly smelling leftovers of human desires. She showed Lucia the old undergraduate class photo (heavily faded) when they met at Analog, a downtown café, twelve hours later.

"This is Vikram Jit. He is dead. But if you read Lila's novel, he is not dead."

Padma had labelled everyone clearly in the photo.

"Have you ever seen this man?"

Lucia could not tell for sure.

Padma also handed Lucia a copy of her undergrad paper that got published abroad. "This man Vikram Jit provided me with data based on a fossil he stole from Professor G's collection. What he did not know was that the professor had already stolen the fossil from elsewhere. As if this were not enough, Vikram Jit also provided me with a photographic image of another fossil (which was a photocopy of an image published by Dr. G) without realizing that the doctor had photocopied the image from a paper published in 1892. This is the same Vikram Jit in Lila's novel.

■ ■ ■

For obvious reasons it would be best to skip the inchoate conversation they had about me.

"No," said Lucia. "I never encountered the person in the photo. But let me look at the photo more closely. Let us keep in touch."

She kept one more thing from her interlocutor, thoughts about her face, which was intense, but hard to read. Padma's hands displayed more emotion than her face (or her monotonous voice); it was as if Padma's hands were her face.

■ ■ ■

That night Lucia tucked her youngest child in bed. She returned to the living room to give some order to disorder. Toys with wheels and twisted body parts and Lego. The TV was on. The program on *Nature* was about creatures who live in the oceans. A scientist (my skin colour) with a shock of white hair was explaining that sound doesn't travel the same way in water that it travels in air. This was followed by the human-induced noise pollution in the oceans and its effect on whales. The sound scientist grew a bit philosophical toward the end. *If I was not allowed to keep both the senses, I would choose to go blind rather than go deaf.*

Lucia's husband was away, which was often the case. The TV program made her think about something she had not thought about for a while now. When they had just met as university students, she had recorded his voice in English and in Hindi. She had recorded her own voice as well. She had translated a passage from the German edition of *Maus* by Art Spiegelman into English, and he had translated it into Hindi, and they had read the texts out loud in German and English and English and Hindi for the recording device, and toward the end, swapping languages, she pronounced *Mein tum se pyar karti hoon* and he pronounced a lusty version of *Ich liebe dich.*

Lucia went to the basement and searched for the shoebox.

It took her a couple of days at a downtown shop to get the dusty cassette tape digitized.

She played it for Padma then during their second meeting at the same café.

"Could the man in the photo be associated with this voice? Perhaps I encountered him briefly when I had just moved to Calgary."

Padma closed her eyes for a long time. She wanted to

say yes but could not say a definitive yes.

Padma kept thinking about the voice she had heard. During her long return flight to India, two changes and a ten-hour layover in Dubai, she regretted not asking Lucia for a recording. But she could always do so via the internet.

An old memory resurfaced in her Gondwana-style study.

She too had old cassette recordings. Dusty like her memories.

She found not one but two with Vikram Jit's voice.

The two of them Skyped.

Both were now able to say a definitive yes.

"Why are your eyes moist?"

"I don't know," she said.

■ ■ ■

A humbling moment for me as a detective. I failed to detect his voice. Now I understood something I could have never figured out on my own. It was Vikram Jit who planted the stolen fossil fish skull in Gauri's backpack. To make her look like a petty thief before the whole department.

Padma and Lucia arranged and had one last Skype chat. It was about Mee-Mann. She had given Professor G the original fossil fish skull, a gift, a token of goodwill, the one he later "found" in the Himalayas. Dr. Mee-Mann Chang told Dr. T, the whistle-blower, that such fossils were so common in China "they were frequently offered to foreign academics and distinguished visitors as gifts." She opened her palm and showed him a nearly identical fish skull. Then another.

> **Mee-mann Chang** (born 1936) received the 2017 UNESCO Award for Women in Science for "her pioneering work on fossil records leading to insights on how aquatic vertebrates adapted to life and land." Several deep time creatures have been named in her honour: the theropod dinosaur—Sinovenator changii, the extinct bird—Archaeornithura meemannae, and the sarcopterygian fish—Meemannia.

The one mystery still hanging, the murder of the lab assistant, was not fully solved. Dr. T had repeatedly talked about the murder in international media. He kept the lab assistant alive at least for a decade. Those days he would also get invites from the Australian public broadcaster, ABC, to participate in programs devoted to whistle-blowing. The twenty-first century began with the Y2K bang and whimper. Dr. T was more or less forgotten. Just like his beautiful short little book on gems and minerals. I used to have a second-hand copy. The Indian booklet on peripatetic fossils made not a single mention of the murder. It took me a while to notice the simple fact: the document was published under the watchful eyes of a prominent palaeontologist who happens to be a close relative of G's thesis supervisor. The aftermath of the G story seems as complex as the original, the kind of complexity that gets resolved only in dreams. The world, India, and Canada will have to live with this hanging thread. Real life seldom resembles a crime novel. Or at least I thought so.

■ ■ ■

Lucia, overwhelmed, needed a break. She drove to a random mall and a random store and got herself an expensive new dress, undergarments, and shoes. She had not bought something for herself for a while now. She spent a long time in the changing room. She thought about her childhood, her first pet dog. She had not forgotten its name.

At around midnight she received a phone call.

A man had found her wallet with all credit and bank cards and her driving licence in the mall parking lot.

The man offered to drive to Lucia's place.

Moved by his kindness, she found it hard to follow the routine. The kindness of a stranger, a recent migrant to the city. She tried to figure why this had happened, why she forgot her wallet there. She opened and reopened it after the kind delivery. In the wallet there was a photo of her husband.

■ ■ ■

He was sleeping in the room that was also her room.

■ ■ ■

She called the babysitter about the next day and slept on a sofa not far from me.

■ ■ ■

This book has seen better days, said the blue-haired checkout clerk at the Calgary Public Library, the new building, where Lucia borrowed *U-Turn*. She read the introductory chapter twice: "Every day, in almost every field, someone perceives themselves on the wrong side of a psychic divide. The 'second brain' in their gut tells them their life must change."

Lucia tried to think clearly about all she knew so far. Compared to me she knew next to nothing. Even if she knew half as much as I had figured out, what proof did she have? Everything was sufficiently ambiguous: all she might be able to show was that her husband had lied to her about his past (for what he thought to be a valid reason).

Of course it was possible to prove that he had published a questionable paper as an undergraduate. He could defend even that matter very easily.

So the whole question was deeply personal.

She struggled over whether to have a straightforward conversation with her husband. She was certain any conversation about his past would change the nature of their relationship. One more thing. To go deeper into his past would make him ask her questions about her own past, and she did not want to go anywhere near that thing, always shifting.

■ ■ ■

During those days of high anxiety, I would look at Lucia and I would hear and see her. She felt something odd in her room especially during my appearances, but I rarely appeared optically. There was sufficient ambiguity; she could always find a reason for what was going on in the room. I would stand near the dinosaur collection of children. At times I would sit down on the carpet, where the youngest had been playing with *T. rex* dinosaurs—some of them twisted in odd ways and some with a leg or a neck or a wing or a tooth missing—always looking at Lucia's face.

During those days I would question the focus of storytellers on human beings. Perhaps it is the objects one should aim to focus on, objects, even our rejected and discarded objects, which continue in our absence. Even in the everyday it is we who enter or leave their lives, not the other way round. The world continues without the continuation of the living, and also the dead.

Lucia started dealing with her anxiety by lighting more and more candles.

Perhaps she was doing it for me. She did not know that I could not and cannot stand the lilac fragrance she is fond of. Those candles of hers (proliferating in mirrors) would make me want to flee, but immensely curious about her life, I would stay put even then, unless there was some emergency.

One night, not able to take it any longer, she broke the cardinal rule of performing textual analysis. She read aloud a passage from my book to Ghosh and demanded politely what it meant to him. For many months now he had the answer ready. "The character commits suicide to save his own life."

"Did he harm someone?" she asked.

"I don't know. The way she has composed this passage he will always be able to defend himself."

■ ■ ■

When a house burns down, we are either inside or outside. If we are inside, we try to save a few things as we flee to safety. If we are already outside, we seriously consider entering the house in order to save something special. What we rarely think about are the things we don't try to save, things we would have saved if the house had burned down some ten years ago, or even a year ago, sometimes just a few days ago. It seems we are glad to let certain no-longer-special things go, things that linger in the corners and basements and wardrobes and cabinets as reminders of a past we are no longer comfortable with, a past we find difficult to face and yet do not seem to find the courage to destroy.

We often forget accidents in life (and in death); we learn to deny that such occurrences, among other things, resolve many loose ends. The future is not future if it can be predicted entirely. Even if we are able to do so, we will have to still leave rooms for the unexpected. I don't know if *rooms* is the right word here. We are so stuck with our languages, our ways of thinking, even when we compose treatises like *The World Without Us*.

One thing is clear. Children will continue to grow, and nature and history will continue to make their aliveness felt, and unexpected mini-asteroids will continue to fall on us and our most stable relationships. And in that sense, nothing will change.

Lucia's eldest daughter, the keen teenager, just finished her first year at the university. She knows she is going to study the survival of corals in tropical oceans. Lucia has still not told her certain things about her father.

It is almost a year today, a year from that day when Lucia drove this daughter (and her other two) to the university campus in a nearby town. Her husband was unable to accompany them because of the flu; Lucia gave him medicines and he lay on the bed right after. To celebrate the occasion, many candles were lit all over the house.

By the end of the day (in the nearby town) Lucia and her children had heard about the unreal event. One of the candles had started a fire; perhaps a pet was responsible, perhaps one candle fell when the door was being shut. I did not witness the scene in its entirety. It sounded like a colloidal slurry flowing through a problematic hose. The police could never locate the exact trigger for fire; as a result the girl's father's death was concluded to be an accident.

A ninety-two-year-old man recycling bottles had noticed the smoke and flames and alerted the emergency services.

The only thing that escaped undamaged was a Manitoba maple sapling the girl had planted by the car garage.

She told her mother she would follow in his footsteps. He was a great scientist. "Yes," said Lucia, admiring her daughter from real close. "Yes, but . . ." And that *but* gave me some hope. More than hope. The fire had engulfed my photo as well—sort of a relief—I thought about a cherished poem my mother used to recite—Dil ke aa'iane me tasvir apne yaar ki, jab ji chaha gard'an jhuka'li dekh'li. *In the mirror of my heart lies embedded the face of my friend; whenever the urge arises, I bend my neck and make contact . . .* For me Lucia's *but*, the but she uttered so naturally, was just an astonishing word; it was her face, her new face, and I can wait for an entire eon to find out where it goes . . . That but, that face, is the beginning of Lucia's novella, and the beginning of the rest of her life, and with that word she will save my story (not a big demand; much less than what I demanded of myself), and the first thing she has to do to save my story is to make corrections to the one floating around. Only then will I depart. And right after I depart, feeling my absence, she will take a deep breath and stare at me using some standard *foraminifera* of a phrasal verb, "Come back."

Yes, but.

Acknowledgements

Anton Kirchhofer, Helmut Weissert, Susan Gaines, Sneha Sudha Komath, Arvinder Singh, Zac Robinson, Kim Nekarda, Bron Sibree, J. Mark Smith, Peggy Herring, Daniela Jansen, Verena Heise, Ivan Tadic, Gema Martinez, Rosa Sundar-Maccagno, Jim Olver, Meg Yamamoto, Derek Pardue, Ann-Lise Norman, Anna Auguscik, Denise Drury, Malcolm Lim, Tanya Handa, Vamini Selvanandan, Ross Glenfield, Sydney Barnes, Kate Kennedy, Tori Elliott, Claire Philipson, and Taryn Boyd.

Das Hanse-Wissenschaftskolleg (Institute for Advanced Study, HWK), Delmenhorst, Germany. Alfred Wegener Institute, Bremerhaven, Germany. Fiction Meets Science (FMS), Bremen and Oldenburg, Germany. Panjab University, Chandigarh, India. University of Alberta, Edmonton, Canada. Banff National Park, Canada. Yoho National Park, Canada. Calgary Public Library, Canada.

Text Credits

p. v: "The Anthropocene will not go away when we go away." (Jan Zalasiewicz; the extract is from a recording of a climate change event at the University of Exeter—*Visualizing the Anthropocene*, 2019).

Other extracts on the epigraph page come from *The Story of the Lost Child* by Elena Ferrante, published by Europa Editions, from *Parable of the Sower* by Octavia E. Butler, published by Four Walls Eight Windows, from *Tomorrow in the Battle Think on Me* by Javier Marías, published by Vintage, and © James Hansen, 2010, 'Storms of My Grandchildren', Bloomsbury Publishing Inc.

p. 1: "Story is our only boat for sailing on the river of time, but in the great rapids and the winding shallows no boat is safe." (*A Fisherman of the Inland Sea* by Ursula K. Le Guin, published by Harper Prism).

p. 15: "If you want to make an apple pie from scratch, you must first invent the universe." (*Cosmos* by Carl Sagan, published by Random House).

p. 129: "Solastalgia" definition comes from *Earth Emotions: New Words for a New World* by Glenn Albrecht, published by Cornell University Press.

p.134–6: Radio interview transcript is from the Australian Broadcasting Corporation archives. *The Science Show* (September 3, 2005). http://www.abc.net.au /radionational/programs/scienceshow/what-happens -to-the-whistleblowers/3368656

p. 224: Source: Wikipedia

p. 226: ©Bruce Grierson, 2007, 'U-Turn', Bloomsbury Publishing Inc.

Further Reading

Barrett, Lisa Feldman. *How Emotions Are Made: The Secret Life of the Brain* Boston, MA: Houghton Mifflin Harcourt, 2017.

Bonneuil, Christophe, and Jean-Baptiste Fressoz. *The Shock of the Anthropocene: The Earth, History, and Us.* London: Verso, 2016.

Chakrabarty, Dipesh. *The Climate of History in a Planetary Age.* Chicago: University of Chicago Press, 2021.

Ghosh, Amitav. *The Great Derangement: Climate Change and the Unthinkable.* Chicago: University of Chicago Press, 2017.

Gould, Stephen Jay. *Wonderful Life: The Burgess Shale and the Nature of History.* New York: W.W. Norton, 1990.

Hansen, James. *Storms of My Grandchildren: The Truth about the Coming Climate Catastrophe and Our Last Chance to Save Humanity.* New York: Bloomsbury, 2010.

Keith, David. *A Case for Climate Engineering*. Cambridge, MA: MIT Press, 2013.

Klein, Naomi. "Dimming the Sun." In *This Changes Everything: Capitalism vs. the Climate*. Toronto: Knopf, 2014.

Lal, Pranay. *Indica: A Deep Natural History of the Indian Subcontinent*. Gurgaon: Allen Lane, 2017.

Malm, Andreas. *Fossil Capital: The Rise of Steam Power and the Roots of Global Warming*. London: Verso, 2016.

Nixon, Rob. *Slow Violence and the Environmentalism of the Poor*. Cambridge, MA: Harvard University Press, 2013.

Reich, David. *Who We Are and How We Got Here*. Oxford: Oxford University Press, 2018.

Shah, S.K. *Himalayan Fossil Fraud: A View from the Galleries*. Lucknow: Palaeontological Society of India, 2013.

Stafford, R.A. *Scientist of Empire: Sir Roderick Murchison, Scientific Exploration and Victorian Imperialism*. Cambridge: Cambridge University Press, 1990.

Talent, John A. "The Case of the Peripatetic Fossils." *Nature* 338 (April 20, 1989): 613–15.

Wenzel, Jennifer. *The Disposition of Nature: Environmental Crisis and World Literature*. New York: Fordham University Press, 2019.

Yusoff, Kathryn. *A Billion Black Anthropocenes or None*. Minneapolis: University of Minnesota Press, 2018.

Zalasiewicz, Jan. *The Earth After Us: What Legacy Will Humans Leave in the Rocks?* Oxford: Oxford University Press, 2009.

About the 500-million-year-old organism on the book cover

Lingulella waptaensis is a centimetre-scale, mineralized brachiopod with a long pedicle. The pedicle keeps the organism anchored to the seabed.

Lingulella is from the Latin: *lingua*, "tongue," and *ellus*, "diminutive." *Waptaensis* is from Wapta Mountain in Yoho National Park. *Wapta* means "river" in the Stoney language.

Lingulella belong to an extinct group of brachiopods that thrived in coastal seawaters more than 500 million years ago. Some brachiopod successors of Lingulella were lucky survivors of the end-Permian mass extinction about 250 million years ago. Ocean acidification and greenhouse climate triggered by excess volcanic carbon dioxide killed off 96 percent of the planet's marine species then. The peculiar phosphatic shell mineralogy of brachiopods made them more resistant to warm, acidic seawater. Brachiopods also survived the end-Cretaceous mass extinction about 66 million years ago.

The artist's impression is by Marianne Collins.

More details can be found at the Burgess Shale Fossil Gallery, Royal Ontario Museum: rom.on.ca/en/the-burgess-shale-the-virtual-museum-of-canada.

A Note on the Author

Jaspreet Singh's non-fiction has appeared in *Granta*, *Brick*, and the *New York Times*. He is the author of the novels *Chef* and *Helium*, the story collection *Seventeen Tomatoes*, the poetry collection *November*, and most recently, the memoir *My Mother, My Translator*. His work has been published internationally and has been translated into several languages. He lives in Calgary. You can find him online at JaspreetSinghAuthor.com.